93

*Don't you ever let no one tell you
to grow up and give up on your dreams........*

*- Musiq Soulchild*

# My Soul Exposed!

Published by *The Studio*
10907 Magnolia Blvd Ste 190
North Hollywood, CA 90601
email: www.jonjonstudio@aol.com

Cataloging -in-Publication Data is on file with the Library
of Congress.
ISBN 0-965-54210-4
First Edition August 2003
10 9 8 7 6 5 4 3 2 1

# Contents

# Acknowlegements

Without a doubt I know if it weren't for God and all he provides this book wouldn't be possible. I praise him. Some of the blessings have come through many people and situations. The Fullilove family. Terry thanks for being there for me. To all my family, my mother, father, my son Jeremy and little boy Nikolas, my sisters Stacy & Nikki, The Newsome Family, I love all of yall! Dwight Newsome, thanks cuz for all your help and support. To my long time friends, who have always been there for me since the beginning of all this, Juan, Kassey, Gerald, Ro Ro, K.B., Peach, and all the boys. Memphis, baby. Thanks!

To some other friendships I have developed, Monica Calhoun, Mikki Howard, Craig Ross, Jean Claude, Jerome and Gordon, Lynn Ross, Dwayne, Mike, Cool Bill, Ron, Khansa, Ty Nichols (thanks for everything), Ernest Thomas, and the many other talented people out here in the land of creative magic they call, Hollywood. I look forward to working with as many of you as I can , so we can create great work!

Lastly, thanks to all the Bookstores around the nation that have supported me.

# Prologue

It was a love that had come full circle. One man. One woman. One child. Who would've thought after a little more than three years, things would get so dangerous and out of control? It's not like Indigo and I didn't already have our share of problems with trying to make our reincarnated relationship work. And what made the whole ordeal even more frightening was the danger it had put our son, Railey, in. To jeopardize his life was the end of the rope for me. I swear, if something had happened to him, I would have killed that bitch, Pam! She was responsible for getting me and my family wrapped up in, of all things...murder. This was all her damn fault! What started out as just a daring affair, soon turned into a terrible nightmare that just wouldn't go away.

In the center of it was me, Jake. Jake Alexander. And why? I'll tell you why; an innocent attraction to a beautiful schoolteacher named Kayra Austin. She was an angel whose relationship with me would prove fatal. Her life of short-lived, failed loves, coincidentally, began long before I came around. Unfortunately, at the time we met and started our yearlong relationship, I was still not the man I wanted to be.

Before we both knew what happened, we'd fallen hook, line and sinker in love or whatever it was we were in. I'll stick to love; at least that's how we felt at the time and shit, who can tell the difference? At any rate, it became evident I would eventually suffer for whatever damage I stood accused of inflicting to her already fragile heart.

\*   \*   \*

Although it was over three years ago, the stench from the end result of it all was still fragrant in the air around me. Nevertheless, tonight I tried not to breath it in. It was Friday and I was with my woman. Happy to be in love with her. Excited she felt the same. It's what kept our lives together.

It had been a long tiring week, shipments of this season's Fall clothing line were coming in everyday, 7:28am sharp. Alexander's was becoming New York's trend setter, since the move from Chicago. Our signature clothes line, *j. Alexander*, was a fresh introduction, 18 months ago, into a mundane market. It caused quite a stir in the industry. During the madness of personal appointments, business meetings, media appearances, blah, blah, blah...my mind frequently drifted to this day I longed for each week. The day that I was able to share with her. No matter how the previous days had gone, we planned and committed to this day. Except this Friday was more special than the others.

We laid quiet and still. Our nude bodies frozen, exasperated from a night of strong, wild and free lovemaking. The sheets underneath us were still wet from the sweat of the passion we'd shared only hours earlier. Neither one of us could believe, in less than a week, we would be *jumping the broom* for the second time. This day would be our last "date day" before we became man and wife, yet again.

The excitement built inside us like a raging river eager to explode into the sea. And explode, we did! Right into, around and on each other. Charge it to the strong love we shared. Charge it to the burning passion inside of us. Charge it to the busy schedules that monopolized our time and kept us from frequently seeing each other. Or charge it to the fact, we weren't living together yet. A decision we made together to avoid getting too comfortable with our renewed relationship, too soon. Whatever it was due to, it helped us maintain an innocent freshness, while we took our time getting to know one another again. Each time we were together felt like our very first time.

When Indigo and I finally emerged from our blissful state, I gently kissed her about the neck to fully awaken her. The affection was returned, and I felt the touch of her moist lips pressed up against mine. I accepted the unspoken invitation to move my kisses further down her smooth, warm, brown body. A choice encouraged by the hand I felt firmly guiding my head between her thighs to her melting pussy. I stayed there and tasted the moist flesh guarding the entrance inside her. She shivered when I firmly captured her ass in the palms of my hands and slowly lifted her, so I could bury my tongue deeper. By now, I moaned at how delicious she tasted to my lips. Before long, we found ourselves intertwined once again.

When we satisfied one another, Indigo escorted me across her huge master suite to the large bathroom, located some fifty feet from the canopy bed. Inside the Roman tub overflowing with bubbly water, we discussed the final arrangements for the wedding, while doing our best to refrain from more sexual distractions. Reluctantly, we concluded there were just too many things left for us to do, rather than to lay around making love all day. Nonetheless, the tub played host to an hour of more slow, playful lovemaking and quick bathing.

Later in the day, we decided to have brunch at a hotel near Coney Island and take a stroll along the boardwalk. By day's end we were back home spending the remainder of the evening making calls and finishing up a few last minute details. Nightfall came before we knew it. By nine o'clock, we had finished what seemed like a manuscript of writing but finally, all the personal notes and envelopes were done. But who's complaining? I was just thankful all of our friends and family would be in Chicago to show their love and give us much needed support. It had been a long time coming for the reunion between Indigo and me. The years of trying to salvage what was left of our crumbling foundation had been difficult to handle. This was mainly due to the fact that the trust in our relationship had withered, as quickly as it came, when we had first set eyes on one another back in '84.

I spent the rest of the night tossing and turning with thoughts of what I could've and should've done, much differently. How I could have been more faithful, shown deeper love, earned more trust and understanding. Looking back, deciding to spend the rest of my life making Jake Alexander, the best man he could possibly be, was the best decision I'd ever made. Because by doing so, I was blessed to be within a week of having my transformation rewarded. With that comfort, I closed my eyes free of worry or concern. In fact, the peacefulness felt so good, I found myself not wanting to spoil it. I just laid there, tangled together with my baby, nakedness over nakedness.

Through the years of pain, trials and joy, we shared a kind of love only two people truly meant to be together could share. The solitude of the night engulfed us like cupped hands holding a fragile butterfly.

We awakened, later in the morning, to phones ringing off the hook. Everyone in Chicago called wanting to make sure everything was still on. Charlotte's call came around ten thirty in the morning to confirm our flight information. She had been the organizer of Indigo's bachelorette party and all the wedding arrangements. In fact, it was her very suggestion that led us to celebrate in Chicago.

# N a k e d 1

We arrived at Midway airport in Chicago around three o'clock in the afternoon as promised on our itinerary. The door opened exposing the jet bridge leading to the gate. My stomach turned with anxiety. When Indigo's hand tightly squeezed mine during the short walk inside the dimly lit and crowded pathway, I knew I was not alone in my feelings. Our eyes met and we gave each other that, 'Are we sure we know what we're doing gaze?' By the time the bright terminal lights peeked through the darkness, we dismissed our moment of doubt with wide smiles and a big laugh, followed by a tight hug that made us both feel at ease.

A small unassuming group of white senior citizens, who were vacationing from a local retirement center in the Bronx slowly dragged up the ramp, holding up the rest of us who were eagerly waiting to get off the plane and go on about our business.

We finally made our way to greet Indigo's longtime friend and prep-school roommate, who was now a newly turned successful corporate attorney for a large Chicago law firm. Charlotte Matthew had done well for herself since the Mission's Girls Preparatory school days, when she stole cigarettes out of her mother's purse and smoked them in the school's restroom. Or shoplifted at the neighborhood flea market and found herself in a county juvenile detention center for an awakening three-month stint. Since then, her path remained straight and narrow.

Once Charlotte spotted us coming through the jet bridge, her arms opened wide. Her smile was brighter than I had ever seen on a person before. It radiated warmth and love, which Indigo and I felt immediately. We returned the love with open arms and enormous smiles of our own.

* * *

Charlotte and Indigo quickly caught up on old times, followed by the status of the arrangements for the party. After a few smiles and grins, Indigo looked at her watch and reminded us that Malik and Nicole's flight from Memphis would be landing soon. They would be riding with us because no one was able to catch up with Eddie. It wasn't a problem. Charlotte had a new big ass burgundy Suburban with plenty of room. Plus, I was excited to see Malik. It had been almost two and a half years since we last saw each other. Mostly, due to Malik's new marriage and my engagement to Indigo, which sent him packing to Memphis and me to New York. And then the rest, I guess, was our need to put some distance between us, as a way of not reminding each other of what happened in the past.

We followed the red arrows to Gate 38, Concourse E, where the three of us shared a laugh after Charlotte spotted the fly of my pants opened, on a day I wasn't wearing any drawers! The red bulb flashed, notifying everyone at the gate the flight from Memphis had arrived. Moments later, the door opened and the passengers poured from the exit like a jailbreak. Just as I expected, Malik and Nicole were the last two to get off the plane, because of his never-ending frugality got them seated in the rear of the plane to save a mere forty-eight dollars. But, forty-eight bucks is forty-eight bucks! I'd heard however, his wife, Nicole, was making some progress in bringing him up from the depths of 'Cheap land.'

When he and I made eye contact from across the crowd, we burst out into a big laugh and practically ran to hug each other. He looked well. His sense of style was better. Much better. He wore a short-sleeve white shirt over a silk red T-shirt. The shirt was tucked neatly inside a pair of black baggy slacks, with a wide belt that had a large silver buckle. And being a shoe man myself, I was very impressed with his selection of black leather sandals that were a dressy casual and fashioned with a cut that didn't show too much of his feet.

I complimented Malik's good taste. He smiled and turned to Nicole to share with her my approval. That's when I saw the large diamond stud earring lodged in his ear. He had always emphatically insisted he would never get his ear pierced, because he felt it was completely out of character for him. Whatever that meant. I called him on the issue. And he said after the summer we'd gone our separate ways, he decided to get an earring as a gesture of our friendship.

I guess I wasn't prepared for an answer like that. And, before I knew it, I felt a big tear welling up in my eye. I extended my hand and Malik snatched it firmly pulling me to him. Nicole joined in and hugged us both. Indigo came, too. Charlotte shook her head like, 'What the hell,' and she moved into the circle of love, taking as many of us under her huge arms as she could. Ahhh!

After our big moment of solidarity, we hurried to find the escalator leading to the downstairs baggage claim. We gathered our luggage, found the truck, packed it, and piled inside. The ride, although through heavy traffic, was pleasant. The one hour it took to make it to Eddie's downtown lakefront condo seemed more like a mere fifteen minutes. We drove to the side entrance located off Lakeshore Drive. The gates blocking the underground garage lifted swiftly once Eddie buzzed us onto the lavish property. Malik and I unloaded our luggage, since we would be the only ones staying. Eddie's home was where the boys were to play for the night. The parties were to be modes of relieving some of the stress and tension. Indigo's bachelorette party was going to be held at Charlotte's north suburban home, just thirty minutes away from the glitter and glamour of the Chicago Loop.

Everyone enjoyed seeing Eddie's place. It had been a long time since any of us saw the lavishly decorated condominium and we all were anxious to check out any new art work or faux painting he might have done. Women loved Eddie's taste, class, neatness, and the attention-to-detail manner in which he ran his life. I must admit, he did keep his home cleaner than any woman I knew. In fact, most women would have found his borderline obsession much too hard to live with. Most did. However, satisfying women hadn't been much of a concern for Eddie since he came out of the closet. He wasn't always gay. How we became friends was a result of a freaky incident, one in which we both ended up dating the same girl back in college. We were members of the same fraternity and he was also a fellow 'wanna be player.' Both of us foolishly ran through as many women as we could, until the pickings soon became slim and the circles of lusts even smaller.

Diana McAllister was a good case in point. She was a cheerleader for our high flying college basketball team and a pretty hot number. Smooth skin, long dark wavy hair, athletic legs, and a Sista's backside. One day, after a canceled game due to a gymnasium fire, I drove Diana home and was to return back to meet her there later for a few beers, a movie and whatever else I could get into!

I got delayed by some of the frat brothers and didn't get back to Diana's place until long after the agreed upon time of nine o'clock that night. When I arrived at Diana's dormitory, her suitemate let me inside, unaware if Diana was even there or not. I had been over there many times before; therefore she welcomed me inside to check for Diana myself. Besides, the girls liked me and knew the purpose of my visits. With my arms filled with a twelve pack of Michelob and a bottle of wine, I made my way to Diana's doorway, which was only covered by a heavy piece of curtain to offer some semblance of privacy. I pulled the drape back without announcing my arrival in order to surprise her with the bottle of wine, which I took from the bag and held in my hand.

I got the damn surprise when I saw Eddie planted deep inside Diana as he held her outstretched legs. She moaned for him to give her more. I wasn't a player hater, but damn! It was my girl! Eddie and I had seen each other before. He was a senior and I a freshman, so we didn't hang together. However, I was sure he recognized my face and knew whose personal play toy he was playing with. I stood in the doorway shaken, but not stirred, as Diana moaned again when he made his way deeper inside her. I guess I deserved this bit of torture, considering the similar scenarios I all too often found myself in. Therefore, my voice remained calm when I alerted Diana and Eddie I was standing there watching them. I spoke almost out of courtesy, not anger. Either way, it didn't matter to Diana. She was in such ecstasy, all she could do was raise her head up, over Eddie's stretched arms, long enough to look me in the eyes and whisper, "Come here." Eddie's strokes were now faster and he looked like he was in rhythm to come. He slowed only enough to look over his shoulder at me as if to ask, "What 'cha gone do?"

He returned to quicker strokes and Diana's head flopped back down onto the fluffed pillow. I smiled shaking my head in disbelief, sat the bag of beer and wine down on the nearby table then walked slowly towards the bed. After a few moments, I felt a warm tingling crawl up my body. I walked towards them just at the point he dismounted. My hand found its way inside my pants, and held the bulge that throbbed so badly, I thought it would explode. Diana turned towards me again and saw my need. She then parted her lips, begging to be fed. I unzipped and freed the anxious member between my legs, holding it firmly with delight, giving her what she wanted and watching her gladly accept it, inch by inch. Eddie meanwhile, dropped to his knees burying his face in her vagina, eating her, licking her like she was his favorite flavor. A long moan escaped from her throat, an involuntary exhaling of pleasure. The rest was interesting, to say the least.

The next morning, Eddie and I shared a laugh about the whole affair. We began to talk and discovered we had a lot more in common than Diana and the fraternity. He was older, so I kind of looked up to him for advice. Also, he was the star player on the basketball team and I loved sports. Plus, when I went through the drama with my first marriage to Indigo he was there for me.

After Eddie graduated, we still kept in touch over the years, but he didn't tell me about his homosexuality until I told him Indigo and I were getting married again. Who knew six months later, days before my wedding, we would be in for the fight of our lives? So, Eddie's 'coming out' was shocking, but it didn't mean a damn thing after a while. This would be our first time seeing him since he'd told us he was gay. When we rung the bell, my biggest fear was I wouldn't act normal around him. Indigo offered a hug and a kiss to calm my nerves, as it appeared I was the only one tripping about the whole thing. Malik, who claimed to be homophobic, didn't seem to be bothered much at all. Indigo rang the bell again. The door opened and Eddie stood at the doorway with a huge smile plastered on his long smooth face. He was a tall handsome man and sharp as a tack.

He greeted each of us warmly, with two kisses on the cheek, after complimenting our group on how jazzy we all looked. He led us inside his fine condo, which was decorated in bright art deco colors and animal skins accented by carefully placed African art and framed prints.

* * *

The party started and the music set the mood, lacing the night with contemporary jazz in the background. Candles flickered to every note around the beautiful entertainment room. The atmosphere was warm and definitely filled with love. When I saw how Eddie made everyone feel at home and comfortable, I was glad he talked me into letting him host my bachelor party. Besides, I'm sure Indigo felt more comfortable with him too because she knew he wouldn't fill the night with heavy drinking and booty shakers.

Indigo and her crew stayed a little while longer with us until they decided it was time to get their own party started. After a final toast with champagne, to good friends, good times and good love, they said their good-byes. Indigo kissed me and wished us fun for the night. I returned the well wish and we agreed to meet at Eddie's house the next afternoon at three. Until then, we were on our own for the night's celebration.

* * *

During the drive home, Charlotte kept the ladies in stitches with details about her current relationship with a fellow attorney named Joseph. They had been seriously dating for the past year, but his stiff ass personality had finally started tap dancing on her last nerve. Later, they would find out some of the things that fool did were as disturbing, as they were amusing.

They arrived at Charlotte's house full of jokes and laughs. Nicole was the first to get out of the truck and she quickly grabbed her things. Indigo followed next and then Charlotte, who led the way inside. She escorted her guests to their rooms. Before congregating in the kitchen to gather the hors d'oeuvres Charlotte had prepared the night before, everyone moved to the living room and planted themselves into position for the night's festivities. It wasn't long before the doorbell rang with guests. A half- hour later, a few other women, a couple who were also old college classmates of theirs, arrived and the real fun began. With the help of plenty of margaritas, the later the night got, the more intense the conversations became.

\* \* \*

It was now eight o'clock and Eddie took the last dish he'd prepared out of the huge red brick oven. The eight-foot-long dining table was set with gold tip silverware, porcelain plates and of course, plenty of candles. In the center was the feast of a lifetime. Eddie had it going on! Broiled lemon-pepper orange roughy, long-grain wild rice, baked macaroni and cheese, fresh collard greens, corn bread, quiche, steak and shrimp. By the time we were finished with dinner, it was almost ten o'clock. Not long after, we began making our way down a path of discussions that would prove to have a lot of drama attached to them.

"Need any help, Ed?" shouted Lawrence into the kitchen where Eddie was carefully washing the dishes.

"No, thanks. I can handle this in here, there's only one or two plates left. What I want help with is, understanding why you guys are trying to talk some sense into Cedric about women. You know his ass is a lost cause," replied Eddie peeking his head around the doorway to see Cedric's expression.

"You got a point there," laughed Lawrence.

"Hold up," Cedric retorted in his own defense. "All I said was, I believe the last female I dated dogged me out for no reason. One day we were so much in love and the next she acted like I was a piece of shit."

"I met her a few times and she seemed to be the one woman out of the others I've seen you with, who could communicate her feelings. If something you said or did bothered her, she would have discussed it with your ass," pointed out Eric in his usual cut-to-the-chase fashion. He was another lifetime member of the crowded, 'men who keep losing good women' fraternity.

"That's exactly what I thought too!" Cedric quickly replied.

"What happened then?" I asked, wanting to know more. I knew from my experience with relationships there were always three sides to every story. His side, her side, and what really went down.

"Yeah, spit it out Cedric," encouraged Lawrence, a smart brother, who had always excelled academically and now was a college professor at Morehouse in Atlanta. Since winning an one point four million dollar lotto jackpot, however, it was his common sense we'd questioned sometimes. A testimony to that fact was his stupidity in letting one of his female economics students seduce him into an eerily codependent relationship. She even convinced him to cosign for her a new BMW convertible. After the relationship went sour, so did the car deal. And in a heartless insult to Lawrence's kindness, she let him know her interest in him was only for material gain.

Cedric was also a proverbial 'good man,' too. But, it was something about the way he presented himself that created an air of desperation. Whenever he got off first base with women, inevitably, he'd end up turning them off. Either he wanted constant reassurance they weren't going to leave him. Or he'd try to wrap them up in a steady courtship before the time was right.

"I told you Negroes, I didn't do nothin' this time," said Cedric.

"This time huh? But you do admit you have been messing up lately," taunted Lawrence.

"Okay, I've had my share of screw ups in the past. We all have! But this time it wasn't me. We did have a conversation at her house the night before I noticed a change in her. In fact, I even spent the night with her. Everything was beautiful. I brought her flowers and she cooked dinner. Later, we had a few drinks, talked, then we went to bed and made passionate love. The following morning, I woke her up very gently and she responded by making love to me again and cooking breakfast.

"Afterwards, she took me back to the train station and didn't call me again," explained Cedric, trying not to get himself worked up again over the issue.

"Well dude, it definitely sounds to me like there is something wrong," Kenny, who was married to Karen, chimed in. "I feel you totally. Women give us this bullshit all the time about how afraid they are to be hurt. Complain they're not being treated right, or that men don't know how to be faithful."

"Women act like we don't have any feelings or emotions. It's always about how they feel," added Eric.

"Yeah, when do our feelings count? It's like they have a free license to stop and do everything in a relationship depending on how they might feel at any given time and then they expect us to just get over it," said Cedric.

* * *

Indigo and her girls were also having a great time. Dinner was catered because Charlotte wasn't much of a cook, with the exception of a few small side dishes she'd learned to prepare, while she was completing her final year of Law school. The food was very good, consisting mainly of Italian cuisine.

When they all were full and ready for more margaritas, they gathered in the living room. Charlotte dimmed the lights and turned the volume up on her compact disc player. Through the small speakers played Eric Benét's song, *Femininity*, a flashback, which sparked reaction from the women like one wouldn't believe. It wasn't long before it became obvious there was some built up issues resting in the hearts of some of those ladies in the room, and this night would prove to be the time when it came out.

"Tarnisha, girl," said Charlotte. "I told you to leave that man alone. He don't mean you *no* good." After her own bitter divorce, she possessed very little tolerance for men.

"What are you talking about no good," replied Tarnisha. "He's about as good as the fool you keep sticking with."

"We ain't talking about me," Charlotte responded. "See that's your problem; always trying to turn things around, instead of concentrating on your own sorry ass life. Now don't make me have to read yo' ass up in here, girlfriend!"

"Start reading bitch! You don't know nothin' about me," Tarnisha said, all worked up. "All you know is what I want you to know. Seems to me you're the one who needs to be read. You got this big ass house, high-profile job, fancy truck and a daughter in a halfway house wasting away her life, not to mention a son who's a crack pipe smoking loser!"

"My family business is just that, my business! You got the nerves to insult me in my house, talking about my children. I worked hard to try and keep this family in tack, by my damn self! It's no hard dick man around here poked up in my face, making promises he can't keep, won't keep, and don't know how to keep. I've been raising kids for over twenty years, being mama and daddy while working and going to school. Unlike, the stank carefree life you live. You don't know what life is yet. When you grow up and get a family of your own, then you advise me on mine...bitch!" With that said, Charlotte got up from her chair and exited the room. Indigo followed her to insure she wouldn't do anything foolish.

Shalamar was the quiet one out of the bunch. She had been in town only a few short days for the summer, while still a student at a college in Kansas City, when she was introduced to Indigo at a business reception in New York with some other classmates for a function sponsored by her school. Indigo quickly took to her and asked if she would accept an offer to be her personal intern for the remainder of the summer. Shalamar quickly agreed to the job and began working for Indigo the following week. Things worked out so well that her relationship with Indigo grew into a big sister, little sister friendship.

She was a bit of a loner with a small family consisting of only a younger brother. Her mother died when she was only nine years old. The death nearly destroyed her and it was her aunt in Chicago, the only other family she had, who came to her rescue and her brother. She taught Shalamar how to be a woman and help launch her brother Bill into manhood. Despite a revolving door of men in her life, her aunt also managed to instill enough responsibility in him to graduate high school and enlist in the Army. Shalmar resisted her aunt's nurturing, but after a couple years she grew to love her as the mother she didn't have in her life anymore.

Indigo enjoyed the role of being a big sister to the young vivacious woman, who reminded her so much of herself when she was that age, not so long ago. Confident, yet vulnerable. Eager to embrace success. Shalamar was only twenty-five years old and still had a lot of learning to do. Indigo was just the woman to help her. Hopefully, she could school her enough to avoid some of the same pitfalls and disappointments she'd encountered. Shalamar's self-confidence suffered in her social life. To help overcome her shyness, Indigo invited her to the party and promised she would have a good time, if she flew in and stayed until the wedding. With all the commotion, she wondered if she had made a mistake.

"Do they always fight like this?" whispered Shalamar leaning into Indigo, who had returned from the back with Charlotte standing nearby.

"Hey, hey," said Indigo. "You're scaring this poor girl over here. This night was supposed to be fun. You two haven't seen each other in almost five years and you still act like you did in school. Stop all this damn fighting. Charlotte. Tarnisha. Stop it right now! I don't know why there's been so much hatred between the both of you. Tarnisha, after Charlotte agreed to let you come celebrate with us, you promised to be on your best behavior."

"I know what I promised. I only came here for you."

"What about the rest of us? We haven't done anything to you," blurted Rachel. "Why are you angry with us?"

"Yeah, why," asked Charlotte, returning from her time out spot. "Don't take it out on them. I'm the one you've got the problem with. I should be putting your ass out! This is Indigo's celebration tonight and it's not fair for us, or should I say for *you* to spoil it for everyone else. Now, sit your little narrow ass down and stuff a slice of Aunt Blare's homemade apple pie in your big fuckin'mouth, so you can shut up!" continued Charlotte, who was now calm since smoking a much-needed, *before I have to hurt somebody,* joint.

\* \* \*

Eddie was finally done in the kitchen and joined the rest of us at the table. We decided we weren't going to ever get to the bottom of what was between Cedric and his lover. Who knows why women do what they do, act the way they act, and feel how they feel? I knew after all I'd been through with women, I didn't have the answers. But, Eddie sure thought he did.

"Cedric, most women are not used to men who have emotional needs. And let me tell you, when you get one, boy does he have emotional needs! It's taken men since the beginning of time to understand women are emotional creatures and those emotions must be nurtured. Our evolution in emotional sensitivity is a recent phenomenon."

"There goes counselor fruit fly again, with all his free advice on women. Hmmm. Wonder why he knows so much? Oops, that's right, a woman knows what a woman wants," joked Cedric.

"Go to hell, prick," Eddie replied. "You'll be beating your little pecker until a woman feels sorry enough to let you smell the poo-nanny."

"Oh, he got you man!" laughed Lawrence.

"I do believe old Ed here has got a point. I couldn't have said it better myself." I boasted based on my long history with women.

"If you ask me, I don't buy it," said Malik, after being quiet most of the night. "It's just another excuse for a lack of the same sensitivity women expect for themselves and should be willing to give us, just as freely as they want it."

"Break it down my brother to like it sho' nuff is," chimed Cedric.

"Shit, Ed doesn't know what the hell he's talking about. When was the last time he had a woman?" questioned Ray.

"Listen at him, Jake," said Eddie with a laugh.

"Apparently, he doesn't know who he's talking to. Boyfriend, I've had more pussy than you've had bad ideas."

"I can vouch for that," I said, smiling at Eddie. "I can cosign on one in particular, Diana!" I shouted, as Ed and I shared a big laugh about my recollection of our first acquaintance.

"Maybe you were some kinda' stud muffin back in the day when you played ball. But see, that's another point. Women are always attracted to fame and money. A broke, attractive woman can still get a drink, dinner, have sex, and maybe even get her rent paid. A broke ass man? Well, all he got to look forward to is a cold meal and a hard dick! His chances of getting with a woman with something going for herself are slim to none," said Cedric.

"That's for damn sure!" agreed Malik.

\* \* \*

"Does he beat you, girl?" asked Tarnisha.

"No. We've had our share of skirmishes, but I wouldn't say he's ever beat me," replied Vikki.

"What would you say then," asked Indigo, sensing there was more to Vikki's story than she revealed.

"Now Vikki, come on and tell the truth. Do you remember last October when you and I were at the kids' PTA meeting?" asked Karen, who apparently had the same thought as Indigo about Vikki's selective memory.

"Yeah, I remember," she answered.

"I hope you also remember what you told me that night," challenged Karen.

"Girl, I don't know what you're talking about," mumbled Vikki just under her breath. Her voice was saying what her words weren't.

"I'll remind you then," Karen said. "You said, 'Larry choked me, grabbed my hair, and threw me to the ground.' Do you *not* remember that?" asked Karen, not really expecting an answer.

"What! Girl, no he didn't...did he?" inquired Tarnisha.

There was a moment of silence, as Vikki gathered her thoughts and tears began to show in her eyes. When she was able to speak, her voice remained low, almost a whisper. The fear was obvious.

"I admit it," cried Vikki. "I do provoke him into doing that, though. It's almost like I wanted him to hit me. I pushed him to do it, but when he wouldn't, I tried harder."

"Girlfriend, please! You're talking real crazy," said Nicole. "Why in the world would you try to get your man to hurt you?"

"As a woman, we all know sometimes we piss a man off on purpose, just to get his attention when their sorry asses start acting like we don't exist or take us for granted," said Indigo.

"But I think I speak for most women when I say we ain't trying to get a beat down. I'll leave his ass first!"

"I guess I wanted to be hurt and feel the pain," responded Vikki with tears still creeping down her face.

"Feel the pain? You need help," said Indigo. Have you had any for this?"

"You're kidding right?" asked Shalamar bashfully, trying not to offend Vikki.

"I wish I was girl. It's not like I'm screaming 'give me a black eye!'"

"What are you screamin' then?" asked Indigo.

"All I'm trying to tell you is, from the I way I find myself acting sometimes, it just seems like that's what I want."

"I hope that's not what you want. You deserve better. I don't care what you've done or how you feel about yourself. He ain't got the right to do it and you shouldn't allow it. If you are doing things to provoke him, it's not right. You're putting yourself in jeopardy and it's not fair to him. Larry seems to love you very much and judging from what I know about him, he's not the fighting kind of Negro at all," Indigo said.

"That's right, Indigo," added Charlotte. "Vikki, we've been your friends for a long time and none of us wants to see you hurt. If you need some help you have to say so. Whatever was or is going on, I wish that you had enough faith in us, your friends to let us know before now. Especially, if you were putting yourself in danger."

"Thank you. Thank all of you," Vikki cried. "God knows I felt all alone. It means so much to me that you guys care. Thank you, God. Thank you."

\* \* \*

Eventually, Ray found the right woman and married Rachel. By then he wasn't right. Therefore, when he spoke about matters of the heart, Ray was passionate in describing his failures in being a man who just wanted to be loved. His tone of voice could have easily been mistaken for anger or bitterness.

"Ray, who is this woman you've been seeing?" I asked.

"What the hell are you talking about?" he asked.

He spoke to me like I was an ignorant fool who couldn't recognize his game from a mile away. He was only twenty-seven years young and had been married to Rachel for almost two years. She was a good woman: intelligent, loving and tolerated most of Ray's bullshit, although her patience was drawing thin.

"Don't be no fool or think for one minute she's one," I said, trying to hammer home my point. "Believe me, my brother, you'll be making a terrible mistake if you do. A big one! Trust me, you don't want to deal with a woman scorned."

"Yeah man, you should have gotten over the need to do all that running around," one of the others said. "Hell, you're only two years into the marriage and you are already screwing up before you've given it time to work."

"You better listen to him boy," chimed in Pops who had been in the bathroom for almost an hour trying to relieve himself from a hard fought bout with constipation.

"Use this head for a change," continued Lawrence tapping Ray's forehead with his short stubby index finger.

"I still want to know who she is," shouted Cedric.

"I don't believe it," I said. "This man is cheating on his wife and all you can say is who is she? Does it really matter who he's losing his family over? Once they're gone...they're gone." I pleaded, even though I was a bit curious myself. Who was Ray seeing and who he felt was worthy of him jeopardizing his family for? I thought to myself.

"Sounds like to me a little R. Kelly is in order," said T.J., who'd been keeping a low profile. "Hey Eddie, I hate to ask because I'm feeling the Miles Davis, but can you play R. Kelly's song, *When a Woman's Fed Up*, for Ray-Ray? I really think he needs to hear it right about now."

"You have got to be kidding," said Eddie. "You want me to take off Miles and put on 'Mr. Bump and Grind' man? Do you know this CD, *Kind of Blue*, is an original Miles Davis 1957 live recording session with Wyton Kelly, Jimmy Cobb, and John Coltrane on sax. John Coltrane! Can you believe that? This is a classic you're listening to."

Eddie's attempt to hip the younger guys to a little culture was a miserable failure.

"Come on, Ed. Just one song," pleaded Eric.

"When will you sweeties ever learn? One song then it's back to Miles."

"Eddie, if you don't like R. Kelly, why did you buy the CD?"

"I didn't say I didn't like him. The music ain't why I bought it. I'm sorry, his ass is just fine!" erupted Eddie.

At that point, I began to feel quite uneasy about Eddie's sexuality. For the first time I heard it! I heard him say he was attracted to another man. I could've put up with his little *funny* mannerisms, because he wasn't a sissy looking gay man. He still was tall, muscular, and had firmness in his eyes, but he wasn't the smooth, aggressive, macho charmer I'd remembered.

Anyway, it would be something I would eventually get over, once I let go of my own hang-ups and just accepted him for who he was. I didn't agree with his choice, but Eddie would have to live with it. Not me or anyone else.

"Here it goes, Ray-Ray," laughed T.J. "You'd better listen to it, or you'll be singing it soon!"

Eddie eventually convinced us to leave Ray-Ray alone after we ended up playing the whole R. Kelly CD. He had grown tired of all the shade tree advice. The truth of the matter was, Ray-Ray was right when he said that none of us had any room to talk. My difficulties with women because of my own bad decisions were well documented, and from what I remembered about the others, they had lives full of foolish indiscretions too.

We stood and moved my little party, turned twelve-step program for the stupid at heart, into the den where Eddie broke out the good stuff. He served five vintage bottles of Italian Chablis dated 1928. He filled everyone's glasses and then presented each of us with a box of Cuban cigars. We toasted to my marriage, love, life and happiness. For good measure, we lifted a round for a life of less stupidity. We lit our cigars and continued sipping the wine. Everyone enjoyed and savored the flavor of both, as silence became sound for the moment. It seemed as if we stared into each of our own circumstances. Reflecting on our special time together.

# N a k e d 2

*ndigo and her girls* opted for less strenuous conversation the rest of the evening. Vikki's sobbing stopped. Through the tears shed that night and the support that resulted, she realized her dire need for professional counseling. Undoubtedly, she was a woman with a deflated sense of self-worth and was suffering from depression.

A new willingness to seek help and the love, encouragement and support of her friends, Vikki was already beginning her healing process. She felt in control of her life again. Attractive, witty, smart "go-getter", who was finding the peace of mind she had been desperately craving throughout her thirty-seven years. Happiness was hers to embrace and not for another to give or take away. Especially, not a man! And vice-versa, she knew she couldn't and wouldn't determine a man's happiness, either.

I liked Vikki a lot. I felt her. There was a time when I

feared being alone, that my worthiness for a happy and healthy relationship had somehow played out like a bad poker hand. I wondered after finding new ways to screw up every opportunity I had to be with a wonderful woman, who loved me and wanted to spend a life together, if there were any more chances left for me. With Vikki's long history of here-today-gone-tomorrow relationships, she and I shared the same matters of the heart it seemed. Although, much of her problem rested with her own decision to remain celibate after her last child was born, a claim I unfortunately couldn't and wouldn't make.

Most of the men Vikki dated respected her lifestyle choice. They proved to be sensitive and understanding, except when it came to Vikki's many other hang-ups. She, on the other hand, seemingly refused to accept their sincerity. In her eyes, they only found her intriguing long enough to wait and see if her panties would drop. There was only one door left to her heart. That one, she'd padlocked and guarded closely. The results were less than outstanding, genuine men who she ran away and pushed into the darkness of her confused abyss.

That was until, Larry. He, by some strange twist of fate, hung in there long enough for Vikki to give him the key to her long locked heart. But, her vows weren't forever like she'd promised at the altar, before friends, family, God and most importantly, Larry. Because of Vikki's nagging insecurities, the marriage became increasingly more challenging. Then came the anger and the physical confrontations Vikki felt she needed in order to prove her worthiness to be loved. It was a complex issue, indeed. The night of the party was just a continuation of the saga.

Shalamar's shyness made her easy prey, as the women redirected their attention to her. Maybe, it was because none of the other ladies, except Indigo, knew this young, beautiful damsel with the long flowing hair and the light brown eyes. Or, maybe they were just plain damn nosey!

"Ms. Shalamar," Tarnisha began, "where are you from, again?"

"California."

"Oh really? What part?"

"A small town southeast of the Bay area called Hayward. It's about forty-five minutes outside of San Francisco or twenty minutes from Oakland."

"Never heard of it. Must really be in the boonies."

"I guess you can say that."

Now that the ice had been broken, all the girls joined in on the quizzing.

Nicole was next. "How long have you been in New York?"

"Only a couple of months. I'm working with Indigo for the summer."

"Are you going back to California when you leave,"

asked Rachel.

"No. Actually, I live in Kansas City now."

"You're a real rolling stone." replied Rachel.

"Kansas City!" Tarnisha yelled in her ghetto way. "What the hell is in Kansas City? Ain't no black folks there, is it?"

"I'm going to school there. And, yes, there are plenty of us in Kansas City. And plenty of barbecues! I see a lot of sistas in town, but I don't have many friends. I'm not much of a social butterfly, I guess. At this point, I just want to finish school."

"Are there any fine brothers?" asked Karen.

"I know that's right, girl," said Charlotte laughing. "I like those young college boys.

"Girl, yo' ass needs to stop chasing those tenderonies before you get turned out trying to get yo' groove back!" Tarnisha could get some good ones in. This crack on Charlotte had them all in an uproar.

"Yep, there are plenty of brothers on campus. Mostly, a lot of dorky looking ones, but I'll admit I have noticed a couple who aren't too bad."

"Well?" asked Karen .

"Well..." Shalamar answered. She wanted to be a part of and accepted by the circle of women, but was beginning to get intimidated and didn't want them to see her sweat. Even though it felt as if it was visibly dripping from her sleeve.

"Have you got a man?" Karen quizzed. "I hope you're not, uh, well, you know?"

"Excuse me," said Shalamar, taken aback.

"Karen!" shouted Indigo, not wanting this to go on any further.

"Well, I just asked," said Karen. "No need to throw the book at me."

"Actually," added Tarnisha, "I thought that too at first. Seemed like she might like a little licky-lick."

"No, I'm afraid not. I don't like pudding that's mine, if that's what you're getting at. In fact, I've recently met a real nice guy I like a whole lot."

"That's good, honey," Karen said. "I was just wondering. You never know these days. Isn't that right, Charlotte?" A smile opened up on both of their faces.

"How much longer do you have until graduation?" Rachel asked. "Are you close?"

"Yes, thank God! I'll be finished in December."

"Then, what?" Nicole inquired. "What are your plans?"

Indigo, with a gentle rub of Shalamar's back provided an answer as she smiled. "Move to New York and work for me, I hope."

"Thank you, Indigo. I just might take you up on your offer and do that. But, I'm considering staying in Kansas City to try making a go of it with the guy I'm seeing."

"That's a big decision," Indigo said. "Are you sure you're ready for that?"

"I think I am."

"Girl, you better know!" said Charlotte.

"He says he cares about me a lot and we were meant to be together. He also said he's never met anyone who makes him feel like I do."

"You believed him?" Karen immediately cast a glance in Charlotte's direction after asking her question.

Rachel shouted, "Sweetheart, you're just whipped!"

"Where's he from?" Indigo hadn't known about Shalamar's love interest.

"Georgia."

"I knew it," Tarnisha blared out as she stood pointing at Shalamar. "A little southern charm and a big country dick will do it every time!"

"You know about that, don't you, Rachel?" she asked, not really expecting an answer.

*   *   *

"Here, Pops," said Eddie. "Take a little of this, it should help you with that problem you got."

"Give me those damn things," smiled Pops, quickly taking the unopened package of Ex-lax from the outstretched hand.

"Ray, when you going back to Florida?" asked Cedric.

"After tonight, I'm beginning to wonder if that's a trip I should be making again."

"Oh, that's where your little backdoor girl is from?"

"Yeah. I mean, no. She's actually from somewhere else. We met down there while she was on spring break and I was in town to cover a convention in Miami."

"I be damn, just like a corporate businessman," said Eric. "Always mixing a lot of pleasure with very little business."

"Anyway," Ray continued. "We bumped into each other on South Beach at a nearby novelty shop. Damn, she looked wonderful that day! It was strange because she had all of this stuff sitting on the counter. But, when she looked in her purse..."

"Don't tell me," T.J. interrupted. "She couldn't find her wallet, right?"

"As a matter of fact, she couldn't."

"Oldest trick in the book," said Eric.

"At that point, I didn't give a damn! I introduced myself. We'd cast glances earlier in the store. Then, I offered to spot her the money, if she promised to return it over dinner."

"Sugar Daddy, Ray," Cedric was quick to jump in. "I can't believe you've gone and hooked up with some chick, who has the big eyes for money."

"It wasn't like that. She didn't want me to pay, but I kept pushing the issue. And, for your information, she didn't even wait until dinner to give me my money back. Instead, she invited me to follow her to the hotel where she was staying. It was just down the block from where we were."

"She gave it up just like that? Not the money, but the booty?"

"No, you fool! I waited downstairs in the lobby until she came back with the money. Afterwards, we hung out together for the rest of the day and then the remainder of the week. The rest, like they say, is history. When the week was over, she went back to Kansas City. And, from then on, we've kept in touch. When I can slip away for a couple of days, I'll go and visit her."

"Does this woman know you're married?" Eddie asked. "Frankly, I think you're playing with fire and somebody is going to get burned real fast."

"I haven't told her, yet. But, my situation isn't about getting laid. Rachel and I have been having problems for a while now. I guess I just fell victim to what's missing at home."

I had to jump in. "Look, I've been there and I know what you're feeling. However, I can honestly say, whatever is going on between you two ain't worth it."

"What's her name, anyway?" asked T.J., our local starving artist in the group. "Who we talking about?"

"What difference does it make?" asked Ray, a little annoyed. "It's not real important. Besides, it's over now. But, if you guys insist on knowing, her name is Shalamar. Shalamar

Davis."

"What?" I couldn't believe my ears and everyone knew it.

* * *

"How did you meet this new love of your life, Shalamar?" Indigo asked.

"A party probably, huh?" Tarnisha butted in. "Take it from me, the club ain't the place to find love."

"That's funny because all of my nightmares with guys came from the ones I met there," answered Shalamar. "But, this was different. Much different. We met at a store in Miami while I was there on spring break."

"Well, what happened, girl?" asked Rachel anxiously.

"We were in line together. And, I must have had a real brain fart that morning because I had my purse, but I'd forgotten my wallet! I was so embarrassed. There were so many people behind us. There I was at the counter with all of my stuff piled up and no money. He saw how 'on the spot' I was. Since we had already exchanged smiles, as well as, a brief conversation while we were shopping; he offered to cover the bill until I could get my wallet."

"That was very sweet of him," said Rachel.

"I know. It surprised me. My first response was 'no' before I could even think about it. But, he kept insisting, and we eventually got out of there with my things."

"Did you pay him back, girl?" asked Charlotte.

"You know she did," answered Tarnisha, though no one had asked her. "She'll learn."

"See, girl, that's your problem," said Indigo. "Always trying to get over. A good, decent man is hard to find. And when we do find one, a woman like you messes it up for the rest of us by taking advantage of him whenever you can. It's not necessary. If the man was nice enough to do that for her, then why would she want to screw up a good thing? Not many men like... What is his name, by the way?"

"Oh, I'm sorry. His name is Raymond. But, he likes to be called Ray-Ray."

"What?" The women looked at Indigo as her jaws dropped.

* * *

The tone for the rest of the evening was set. Who would have guessed two people from totally different ends of the country would have a secret affair and unknowingly travel within the same circle of friends? Then find themselves in nearly the same place, at the same time with me stuck in the middle! Why all of this had to manifest that night, God only knew.

There was more than enough drama to go around for everybody. Many of us had traveled hundreds of miles to share this night together. Now, the night reeked disaster. This because of the infidelity of an unhappy husband and an unknowing young mistress who just wanted to be loved!

I almost resented Ray for his actions. When I informed him his secret lover wasn't a secret anymore, she was sitting in the same room with his wife, thirty minutes away, I did it with little remorse.

After we lifted him off of the floor, Ray staggered to the door in an attempt to flee for his life. We all stood drowned in shock, at least all of us, but T.J. He seemed to enjoy watching the chaos and was amused by the stupidity of Ray's choice of women. I tried to shut T.J. up and simultaneously calm down Ray, who was so weak he couldn't turn the doorknob to yell for help.

You see, T.J.'s attention span, for matters other than his artwork, was about as short as the jobs he kept. His disinterest began the year before, after his paintings were rejected for display by a prominent gallery located on Chicago's South Side, because of what they deemed as, too surreal. His work was often beyond what most collectors considered erotic, at times it bordered on pornographic obscenity for the average art enthusiast. But, it was the edginess of the scenes and taboo positions masterfully accentuated by the use of vivid colors with broad swinging strokes that gave his paintings the passion he felt should be in art.

The rejection was not new to T.J. He had been turned down many times before. This time though, the Chicago gallery's refusal to display his work came a week after the same curator had praised him for his vision and intensity. Then, two days before the delivery, there was a message on his answering machine.

*This message is for Mr. Terrance Jones. Mr. Jones. Hello. This is Helen Merimore from the Artists Collective Gallery. I'm the director of Public Affairs. I've reviewed the samples you left. As I understand, Nancy Schlomberg approved your entire line for a display run and a private auction. Sir, I'm afraid our arrangement with you will be voided, effective immediately. We're not in the business of alarming our patrons. I've consulted with several other members of our board, and we've all concluded there won't be a place for your work here at this time. All the best to you, Mr. Jones. I'm sorry. Good day.*

The disappointment cut deep and it was jagged. It was not only a financial disaster, as each of the pieces were expected to go for a cool ten grand. Also the termination came just as T.J. was on the verge of accepting and really believing in himself as an artist, trusting his neurotic talent for art. Then came the reluctance to share his talents with the world. Since that time, T.J. had stopped painting and said to hell with everyone.

* * *

Eddie had become the pillar of stability for the moment. He suggested Ray take a moment to sit down and try to make a wise decision about how to handle the matter, instead of compounding the problem by doing something irrational. Well, it was too late! The phone rang, and the echo of each ring seemed to last for an hour, as it faded into infinity. We froze immediately. It continued to ring for three minutes, then five. The air rushed out of the room leaving us breathlessly silent.

Finally, it became obvious the rings weren't going to stop until somebody answered the caller's cry to be heard. The message was very clear: the caller would not be ignored. To do so would be suicide and an invitation for a possible lynch mob of women to come stomping through the door. I made the first approach towards the receiver beating T.J., who was still showing signs of trying to do everything he could to further instigate the situation. He stood next to me with a silly ass smirk on his face. I didn't know whether to push him away or to just overlook his juvenile behavior, which could've been only due to his carefree nature as an artist.

Eddie still remained calm, but he began speaking in a more rambunctious manner, that was reminiscent of the way I'd remembered him several years earlier. His voice brought life back into the room, as the music faded and the last song on the compact disc finished playing. "What in the hell are you waiting on?" asked Eddie.

I stood there staring at the vibrating black phone with the green light constantly blinking. It flashed each time that the long rings went unanswered.

"Here goes nothing!" I slowly reached for the receiver,

cutting my eyes to meet those of Ray, who stood with his back against the door and his head buried in his shaking hands, as he peeped through them.

"No," he shouted. "Don't answer it!"

"Time to face the music, boy," said Pops.

"I bet that *pootang* don't seem so good right about now," T.J. said as ruthlessly as possible.

"Shut up, T.J.!" I demanded. I couldn't take anymore of his cavalier attitude.

"What are we going to do?" Eric asked.

"We ain't going to do a damn thing," answered Eddie. "Ray, you'll have to handle this like a man and face the responsibility alone. Like I said earlier, you are playing with fire."

"Man, Rachel is going to kick your ass and your girlfriend's ass," said Cedric. "Sho' nuff'!"

I knew Cedric was right. Rachel had been known to have a lot of spunk. She was from the Bronx and her childhood could be described as one filled with hard knocks. She grew up with both parents in the household. Her countless cases of outright disobedience couldn't be attributed to a broken home. Her father was a tall, burly man and he ruled with an iron fist. This, of course, being no doubt necessary with one daughter and four older knucklehead sons to keep in check. The boys lived for constant mischief and endless fighting with the other neighborhood kids. Rachel soon began to follow in the example of her brothers. By fifteen, she had become the designated "bitch beater" of the family gang. Her father and mother did manage to minimize the incidents as best they could. None of the boys found themselves in jail or involved with any other stuff, like drugs or gangs. It was just a matter of too much testosterone in the house, led by their father who'd also had a hard upbringing in Alabama. When needed, he would kick a little ass himself, most defiantly whenever his boys were threatened by other parents for being too rough on their children.

With a family history of ass kicking everywhere, it was no wonder Rachel, a successful business owner with two hair salons and the mother of a beautiful daughter, could still bring the funk when absolutely necessary. A fact she demonstrated last year when a customer refused to pay for a hairdo, which took over three grueling hours to finish. The lady's only explanation had been she'd changed her mind once she saw it; it didn't 'look right' on her. Then she cursed out Rachel after criticizing her skills as a stylist. A mistake the lady would not soon make again. Rachel beat her down and snatched every strand of weave out of the lady's head, sending her out of the door crying and bleeding from the attack. Therefore, as I lifted the phone slowly off of the hook, I honestly didn't know what to expect. But, the one thing I did know was Rachel was certainly a force to be reckoned with. God only knew what had happened to Shalamar at Charlotte's house!

"Hello," I answered with a low mutter. In the background I heard the loud shouting of angry voices and a violent struggle.

"Stop!" A cry sounded before the phone dropped to the floor and bodies could be heard trampling on top of it.

I pressed the speaker phone button, as the rumbling continued for several minutes. The guys gathered closely around the phone, to hear what was surely only half of what Ray could expect to happen to him.

"Bitch, I'll kill you!"

"She didn't know, Rachel." It was Indigo's exasperated voice I heard, as she struggled to pull Rachel from atop Shalamar.

"Whore! How could you?" Those shouts followed a smack which we heard clearly enough to cause us to jump away from the phone shaking our heads.

The rumble resumed and more crushing punches were thrown, accompanied by thundering bangs against the door.

"Damn!" We harmonized together, putting our ears even closer to the phone. Finally, there was one loud crash along with a painful yelp. Afterwards, there was frightening silence. We listened with our ears glued to the line for a hint of what'd happened and the nature of the sudden stillness.

As if she'd heard our panting through the line and read our minds, hands moved about the phone and a trembling voice spoke. "Jake?" It was Indigo. I quickly picked up the receiver.

"Yeah, baby it's me! Is everything all right?"

"I'm okay, I guess. I don't know if I can say the same for Rachel. She's...she's...she's not moving. And there's blood everywhere."

"Oh my God!" Not again, I immediately thought. We've been through the hell of one murder. And now, my wife to be could be caught up in one. This couldn't be. "Is she breathing? What happened?" I tried to ask calmly and not flip out. "Did you do it?"

"No! No! Baby!"

"Whew! Thank, you Jesus," I said with a sigh of relief.

"What? What?" The guys had grown impatient and anxious, as they crowded beside me, since I held the receiver.

"Hold up," I said. "This is Indigo. She's trying to tell me what happened." Turning my attention back to the phone, "Go ahead, sweetheart. Tell me what happened."

"Rachel went crazy when she found out Shalamar was seeing Ray."

"It stung the hell out of us, too, when we found out tonight." I said.

"Well, she jumped on Shalamar, and I barely got her off before she would've killed her. Rachel called over there to talk to Ray, but instead she dropped the phone, then went off again. I guess Shalamar had decided she had taken enough, and managed to get hold of a vase while Rachel was on top of her. She slammed the vase on Rachel's head and she dropped like a truck hit her. Wait! Wait! I think she's coming to. Hold on!"

I used the moment to quickly brief the eager ears and the bad breaths that hovered around me like a cloud of smoke.

"Rachel has a pretty nasty cut," she continued. "We've got a towel pressed against her head to stop some of the bleeding. Charlotte called the ambulance. It should be here soon."

I turned to Ray to assure him his wife was going to be fine, and she would be going to the hospital to get her injuries taken care of. Once he looked like he was settling down, I tried not to, but couldn't keep myself from smirking at the thought of little petite Shalamar knocking out big, rough and tough Rachel. I wish I could have seen it for myself. Not that I had anything against Rachel. But, generally, I'm a sucker for the underdog.

"I'm glad she's going to be all right," I told Indigo. "When I heard about Ray and Shalamar, I feared something awful would happen. Thank God you didn't get hurt in all of this. Get Shalamar out of there now! You hear me? Right now before Rachel gets back on her feet and something else bad happens!"

"Okay, I will. Where do you want me to meet you?"

"Just come here for now. We'll decide what to do next then."

"Baby, we're on our way. I'll get a cab and everyone else can stay here to wait for the police and the ambulance."

"Come on. Hurry! I love you."

"I love you, too, baby."

\* \* \*

By night's end, Indigo and Shalamar had made it safely to Eddie's house. Ray left and was speeding to Victory Memorial, where Rachel was admitted with a concussion and a busted forehead. She needed twenty-three stitches.

Shalamar did a pretty good job of protecting herself, not letting Rachel completely dust the floor with her ass. The rest of my friends stayed and listened to Shalamar protest the whole event, although she herself found it difficult to blame Rachel for her reaction under the circumstances. The black eye, swollen lip, and several bruises, however, made it hard to forgive her.

Indigo did her best to support and comfort Shalamar. Eddie made hot tea out of some Dr. John's Warts to help her relax. But, his nerves were the ones on edge. I'm sure he sat and wondered how his peaceful home, which was always full of love, had turned into a madhouse. It was a crazy night. Little did we know it was only the beginning of what was to come.

\* \* \*

The phone rang again. We all sat as quietly as we possibly could trying to gather ourselves. It was as if we could feel the horror through the rings. A stiff chill ran through each of us. And like before, there was the first ring. Then a second. By the third and fourth, we looked at each other with an unspoken consensus of 'don't answer it.' I wish that it could have been that simple!

# Naked 3

The moment of truth swiftly came. Any one of us could've answered the phone. But, none of us wanted to face the prospects of doing such an act for fear of what we might hear. As of yet, another silent opinion poll had been taken, electing me the best man for the job, there was a collective call of my name. I heard the voices loud and clear, with an unmistakable understanding of their meaning. I took a deep breath, said a quick mental prayer and walked reluctantly to the ringing black phone.

"I don't know why we're tripping in the first place," I said. "This is probably just Ray calling from the hospital." I was trying to convince myself, and the others, this was the likely scenario. "Hello."

"Yes, Mr. Alexander, please," spoke a man with a slow and deliberate deep voice seasoned with a hint of a British accent.

"This is Mr. Alexander." My knees were shaking something awful. I wondered if he was able to tell. "Who is this?"

"Has it been that long, Mr. Alexander?"

"That long? Who is this?" I struggled to recognize the stranger, whose voice sounded all too familiar to me.

"I'm sure you remember three years ago here in Chicago? You know, the murder of Demetria Taylor? Does that refresh your memory, Mr. Alexander?"

"Damn!" I shouted aloud, contemplating hanging up the phone. It was already dangling by its cord, inches from the floor. When I'd gathered myself, I picked it up again and tried to speak.

"Yeah, Detective Hall. I remember you. What do you possibly want with me? And how did you find me here? We just got into town tonight."

"Mr. Alexander, you disappoint me. We've been keeping our eyes on you ever since the day you left the precinct. I hoped by now you would have realized it's not over. No, Mr. Alexander, it's definitely not over. At least, not yet."

"Not over? What the hell are you talking about, not over? It's over for me. I was cleared of all of that."

"Mr. Alexander, again you disappoint me. Tsk, tsk, tsk. Our investigation proved what we wanted it to prove."

"Look, what the hell do you want with me? I know I

haven't done anything wrong. I don't know anything, and I don't have anything. Therefore, sir, we don't have anything more to say to one another. Good-bye, Detective Hall."

"Mr. Alexander, ahh, ahh, ahh. I wouldn't do that if I were you. We have lots to say to each other. Beginning with where the diary and the video are."

"What diary? What video?"

"You could stand a refresher, I see Mr. Alexander. Three years ago, you were caught dab in the middle of my employer's affairs we had to clean up."

"You killed that woman! I was looking for Kayra when she found me standing over her body at Pam's house that night." I said boldly. It occurred to me if they killed Demetria, who was Pam's lesbian lover, then they probably...

"Let's put it another way, Mr. Alexander. She was a slut who was in the wrong bed that night. And before you ask, that's if you haven't figured it out by now, we had to get rid of your little girl toy, too!"

"Kayra!" I shouted. I could feel the tears forming. I was speaking to her murderer.

"Yes, Kayra. She should have picked her friends more carefully. It's not as though I actually did it without prior warning. I told her to stay away from Ms. Johnson."

"Pam, too?" I thought.

"That's the little lady whore, who has been the nuisance

and the thorn in my employer's side. She stole the diary and video from him, and we can't find that tramp or his property anywhere. This is where you come in, Mr. Alexander. You're going to help us find her. We thought you'd been kind enough to lead us to her by now. My employer still wants to quiet her for good. But, apparently, Ms. Johnson seems to have nine lives."

"Damn it, man! What do you want me to do? I don't know where Pam is, nor do I even care."

"My suggestion to you, Mr. Alexander, is that you begin to care. Let's face it: you have proven to be the common denominator in all of this. You knew Pam, Demetria and you were involved with Kayra. We know you, Mr. Alexander. No, in fact, we own you. You will feel our wrath. All of you, which includes your other jigaboo friends."

"What! You..."

"Come now, Mr. Alexander. Have you no sense of humor? Don't be so touchy. You will find both our property and Ms. Johnson or else. Just so you're clear on the consequences, be at Navy Pier tomorrow night at seven o'clock sharp. Alone. Oh, don't forget to tell your friends that you have their fates in your hands."

"Wait a minute!" I couldn't get one word in.

"I've now grown weary of your blabber. Be a good boy, Mr. Alexander, and meet me tomorrow. And, a good day to you, sir!"

I held the receiver for at least another fifteen minutes, in an attempt to ignore the bombardment of questions from the others. How could I begin to explain to them not only was my life now hanging in jeopardy, but so was theirs! I slowly moved the receiver from my ear and eased it back onto its cradle. Desperately, I searched for the appropriate words to say. I gasped after each attempt I made to speak. It was painful, but necessary. I had to do it.

"Jake, sweetheart, talk to me," Indigo said lovingly, trying to comfort me. "What about Kayra? Who was that? Baby, you look as if you've seen a ghost."

"No, but I heard one!"

"Boyfriend, what are you talking about," Eddie asked. "Was it Ray? Is that what's wrong? Is Rachel all right?"

Finally, no longer finding the situation a joke, T.J. commented, "I don't know why, but my heart is pounding like a jackhammer."

"Mine, too," said Shalamar, who had been sitting quietly thinking about her own mess.

"Baby," cried Indigo. "Say something. You've got me and the others scared to death."

"You should be!" I replied before I even realized the weight of my words. They fell from my lips like drops of rain before I could think to catch them.

*   *   *

I didn't know at the time whether the meeting at Navy Pier would be one I'd return from. Detective Hall and his cronies were very dangerous. Even worse, they could hide behind the law to cover up whatever they might do to us. Until we could find Pam, Indigo arranged for Railey, who was visiting his grandmother for the summer, to continue to stay with her, to keep him safe. She had family in a small town outside Cleveland. Under the circumstances, it seemed like the best place to hide. Originally, he and his Nann-na, as he affection-ately called her, were going to fly to Chicago for the wedding. But, that trip was not going to happen. I was not willing to risk his safety.

With our son out of harm's way, Indigo refused my insistence she and the others also leave for their own safety. Her rationale was the murderers already knew where we all were, and it would be only a matter of time before Detective Hall and his people would come to get us. Eddie also dismissed my plea and stood firm with his decision to stay and not be driven from his home. Malik was down with whatever. I think he felt he had been a little punkish the last time we were involved in this mess and he wanted to prove that he had my back. Without a second thought, his wife, Nicole, just like Indigo, exemplified the essence of a virtuous and supportive woman. She chose to stay behind with her husband, Malik. Even Shalamar, as much as she had gone through, decided to stay. Maybe in some strange way the danger thrilled her. She had already proven to me she had a lot of fight in her. They say the quiet types are the ones you have to watch out for. Kenny and a few of Indigo's girlfriends left that night. I was a bit disappointed in a way they hadn't stayed. I couldn't blame them though and I wasn't mad at 'em.

By sunrise, Charlotte and the remaining women at her house called. None of them were aware of my ordeal when it initially poured into my life three years prior. Those of us involved chose not to share it with anyone else-until now. I had a gut feeling regardless of how removed anyone else might have been from the disappearance of the diary and video, no one close to me would be safe. Therefore, it was my obligation to tell them the truth about the sordid chain of events. Charlotte relayed the consensus of the house. Everyone wanted to stay and help with protecting his or her own life. Even with the unwavering solidarity, which was genuine, I still felt no comfort in the gesture of support. I knew there was a strong possibility nothing would really matter. In the end, we would all be killed.

# Naked 4

It was six o'clock. Night had fallen. The cab driver confirmed my destination by pointing to the huge Ferris wheel at Navy Pier. It could be seen while driving along Lake Shore Drive. Why Detective Hall wanted to meet in a public place, flocked by people, was beyond me. I didn't know whether to feel relieved, or more frightened he would so boldly confront me out in the open, as a display of just how dangerous he was. Apparently, he wasn't afraid of my potential to tell passersby about the real nature of our acquaintance.

As the taxi screeched to the curb, just missing two pedestrians and a fire hydrant, I glimpsed through the small crowd looking for Detective Hall. The driver's outstretched arm reached over the torn leather seats of the old Chevy Impala, which smelled like a bag of week old dirty laundry. I slipped a fifty in his hand and dismissed his weak and feeble attempt at finding change. My exit from the vehicle was swift, my attention focused on the real matter at hand.

I approached the strip with slow and calculated steps focusing on the entrance gate of the Pier. I turned over my left shoulder looking towards the street to see if I could spot that asshole coming. I turned back around and there he was, practically breathing in my face. He was a tall, stout man with a firm face and beady eyes. Under his thick dark eyebrows, I saw a long, jagged scar on the left side of his face near his temple. It ran just underneath the socket of his eye to the corner of his mouth.

"Mr. Alexander," he said in a low mumble, as he firmly grabbed my shoulder. I winced at the sharp pain I felt shooting down my arm. "Follow me." The relief from my shoulder being unhanded was welcomed as we walked rapidly towards the slow turning wheel. I had been down there several times before to ride the party yachts, to shop, watch the people and sometimes just to look at the beautiful skyline from the pier. Amazingly, out of all those many visits, I can say with certainty, I never found myself compelled enough to ride that Ferris wheel.

Why over the years I avoided it was beyond me. I always knew one day I would try it. Who would have known my first time could've ironically been my last!

Detective Hall casually leaned over and whispered something into the attendant's ear, average height man , who looked like a child by the face. He was casually dressed in khaki

READING

pants and wore a tight fitting, canvas baseball cap that smothered his head and covered his eyes in an obvious effort to hide his identity.

Ready for whatever might be next, I remained visibly cautious during the quick exchange of words and I stood firmly planted in my defensive posture, a combination of ghetto alley and Tae-Bo.

A slight nod from the waywardly attendant was acknowledgment of his instructions. He maneuvered the switch inside the small control station and the gate opened. Then the wheel stopped abruptly and Detective Hall smirked as he walked towards me with his chest stuck out like a peacock. He seemed satisfied by the accomplishment.

"Relax, Mr. Alexander," he said. It was so nonchalant, like he really expected me to seek comfort in the words of someone, who tried to hem me to a murder rap and had come back into my life  with threats on family, my friends and me. Please!

"We're going for a little ride, Mr. Alexander. Ever been on the wheel?"

My tension rose to a point of no return. I forced my lips to answer the detective's stupid ass question. "No, and I'm not starting now!" My fist balled and my muscles tightened.

The blow struck lightening quick, center mass and flush with his nose. I heard it break. Felt the blood as it splattered onto my cheek. I hadn't hit a man in years; there was no reason to. This time though, it was a matter of life and death. The damage wasn't a pretty sight with the detective having crumbled to the ground, I bought myself enough time to get the hell out of there! My heart felt like it would burst, after the first minutes of running. I felt the tingling in my chest become more intense. The burning in my legs, just moments earlier, now felt like flames. My breath quickened and the oxygen cheated me everytime I inhaled.

Malik showed up from out of nowhere. He drove over the curb, hit a small bush and then stopped midway onto the walkway leading to the pier.

The attendant was getting closer, now that he had left Hall by himself bleeding on the sidewalk. He was fully committed to catching me. Malik opened the passenger door and shouted encouragement for me to keep running. I was so tired. I was nearly fifty feet from the black Range Rover when I heard a loud shot and felt the cement splattered at my feet. It was from a bullet, and the sound propelled me into another gear. My strides were longer and my knees kicked higher. I doubt if I would have bent a blade of grass.

Malik was about to run around to the front of the truck. But he was forced to return back, in order to duck for cover from a second shot that rang in the air. Then there was a third. As the crowd screamed, a stampede began. Again, bullets just barely missed my feet. When I heard a bullet whistle past my right ear, I staggered along in fear knowing they intended to kill me. Everything I passed was a blur. I barely saw the red brake lights that were quickly approaching me. It was Malik. He'd managed to get back inside of the truck, throw it into reverse, and slam on the gas. He backed on top of the sidewalk and met me, just before I collapsed from exhaustion.

"Get in!" he shouted to me, pushing open the passenger door wide enough for me to fit through it. He then reached over and grabbed my shirt pulling me inside.

Another bullet hit the door handle as I slammed it. Malik threw the gearshift into drive and slammed on the gas once again. We swerved just in enough time to avoid more shots.

"Damn! That was close," I said looking at Malik with a closed lip smile to show my relief from the sling he'd just gotten my ass out of.

"I knew it would be. As soon as you left the house, I got Eddie's truck and came down here in case you needed a little backup."

"That's an understatement!" It felt good to have a true friend to count on.

I leaned my sweat soaked head back on the seat, fighting to catch my breath. My legs were still blazing from the two hundred or so yards I'd ran.

"What now," asked Malik, still speeding as fast as he could down the one-way street leading to the interstate. It was our fastest route out of there.

I collected myself and tried to rationalize the crazy thoughts going through my head.

"I don't know," I replied, looking back to make sure we weren't being followed. "Just keep driving."

* * *

"No, sir. Mr. Alexander wasn't dealt with as you instructed. We will get him. That bastard broke my nose!" Detective Hall wheezed and the threat of another nosebleed lurked with each breath. To clear his nasal passages, he hawked thick clots into a small matted handkerchief.

"I wouldn't be concerned about a broken nose, Detective Hall. Screw up again, it might be cut off the next time, if you don't get the job done. Now find him, damn it!"

"Senator Morgan, sir," Detective Hall called to his boss. "Do you still require them to be disposed of?"

"Not yet. So far Detective, you've failed in your attempts to locate Pamela and to apprehend this Jake character. I'd be lying if I didn't tell you I was beginning to doubt your competency."

"Sir, it won't happen again. We'll get him and make him talk."

"Detective Hall, this is not 1928 Harlem. You can't

snatch people off the streets and shoot them in broad daylight through a crowd. I will be a presidential candidate very soon. I can't have your actions traced back to me. Discretion is the key. Is that understood, Hall?"

"Yes, Senator."

"Very well, then. Now, we must employ a different strategy."

The Senator was a handsome fifty-two-year-old man. He was of medium height and sported a reddish tan, which he maintained with his frequent visits to Ft. Lauderdale where he kept a summer home. His light hazel eyes were cold as steel from the corruption, which flourished around him. He had been one of the youngest members of Congress when the people of Illinois elected him to his first term.

After two more consecutive terms with an impeccable record, he ran for a Senate seat and won by a landslide. During his first year as Senator, he was forced to repay favors he'd received along the campaign trail from the mob and other underground corruption cells he courted. Thus, began a crooked political life of payoffs, bogus deals and enough sexual misconduct to put twenty members of Congress behind bars for life. Now, after completing his third term as a Senator, he was trying to cover up his dirty tracks in order to toss his name in the hat for the upcoming Democratic presidential primaries. He had long forgotten about the raunchy and potentially damaging video of him, Pam and his frequent homosexual lover. At least, until a note mysteriously surfaced across his desk about the diary and the video. Later, the delivery followed by an anonymous call, to confirm the proof of his secret past sex life and that it was going to go public.

Morgan pushed himself from the huge mahogany desk. He reached inside his hip pocket and pulled out a single key. A small one was attached to a short chain, which went around his belt loop. He walked to the far wall and inserted the key underneath a small-framed picture. The lock clicked and the door swung open exposing a hidden steel gray safe. Slowly he dialed the combination: Right, fifteen; Left, thirty-eight; Right, twenty-one; and Left, seven with each turn he thought of how stupid he had been to video tape the night of wild sex with Pam after meeting her at a fundraiser a month before.

The door was now released. He pulled it back and reached inside for the small pile of documents and stacks of folders. He quickly retrieved them and swiftly pushed the safe door shut. After spinning the dial and putting the picture frame back in place, it looked as though nothing had been disturbed. His hidden security chest was secured. Afterwards, he walked to Detective Hall who had been standing quietly, trying not to pay too much attention to what was going on.

"Here," he said, slamming the folders onto the desk. "This is how you're going to handle this situation. These are the files I told you about. They contain all the nasty details about all those kids who are making my nights restless. Before I hired you for what I thought would be, need I say, a much more subtle approach to recover my property, I had a little research done. I had one of my agencies do what we call in Washington, a 'scrape'.

"What's that, sir?"

"Basically, it's digging up in someone's ass from the time they were born, to the time they took their last crap. I don't do it often because it's a very expensive process and requires a lot of manpower. But, after Pamela's disappearance, I ordered one knowing it would probably come in handy. This is, as you already know, an extraordinary situation.

"Yes, Detective Hall. The past can be an ugly prelude to the future. Everyone at some point in his life, even you Hall, wants to put the past behind them. Forget who they were, what they did or what was done to them. Well, here's enough history to make Mr. Alexander and his people beg me to hide each of their ugliness. Send each of them one of these. Their names are on the folders. Let each of them know, unless the diary and the video surfaces before the presidential primaries next week, they all will sink. They all will die. And before they do, everyone will know about what I found. Do you understand, Detective Hall? Have I made myself perfectly clear?"

"Yes, sir. Indeed, you have. We'll make sure they

understand. You can count on that!"

"I hope so, Detective Hall. But, make sure you don't forget you are a Chicago policeman and must be discrete. I'll expect to hear from you as soon as you make contact. Damn it! I've worked too hard getting this far to let a bunch of shiftless niggers ruin everything. With them dead or alive, I will be President of the United States of America. President Morgan. Has a nice ring to it, eh, Hall?"

"I won't let you down, sir."

"I would certainly hope not, for your own sake. Now, take those and get out of here."

"Very well, Senator. I'll be in touch with you soon."

"Good night, Detective Hall."

"Good night, ouch, Senator" he cried. Feeling a sudden sharp pain in his tightly bandaged nose, Detective Hall couldn't quite utter everything he wanted to say to the Senator. That was probably a good thing.

* * *

We got enough distance to make me feel a little more at ease, at least for the moment. I exhaled silently to calm my shaken nerves. I didn't react well to bullets. I was allergic to them. I'm sure the others were too. Therefore, whatever it took to keep us from physical harm, I was prepared to do.

We had gotten about twenty miles south of the city near Gary, when I instructed Malik to turn us around. He got off at the next exit and we headed north back towards the city.

"I'm sure everybody is worried to death about us. Especially Indigo who is probably on her knees praying right now."

"I know. I'm thinking Nicole has got to be going crazy."

The conversation between us the rest of the way back, was kept to a minimum. I'm sure we thought about the same thing. What was next, once we got back to Eddie's place?

\* \* \*

"Girl, what has your husband gotten us into?" asked Tarnisha.

"He's not my husband yet, thank you very much. And, girlfriend, I don't even know if I'm sure of what's going on myself anymore." Indigo replied.

\* \* \*

The night before, I began explaining what this whole mess was about. How all of them got pulled into the drama. Before I unraveled all of the unsettling details, however, I stopped because I didn't want to make statements about problems without having any solutions. Therefore, I retreated and left everyone more confused and scared. I felt terrible about not having come up with a game plan. A plan that would get Hall and his people off our asses for good.

Although I was scared as hell of going out to Navy Pier, I didn't expect the slick, cowardly ambush that I'd gotten.

Whether the attempt was in earnest or just an intense warning didn't matter. The line had been drawn in the sand, and it was time to get on the offensive. That sounded good, but it would prove a lot more difficult as we would soon find out.

\* \* \*

As we approached the city on our way to North Michigan Avenue, we could see the glistening skyline in the distance. We were still trying to avoid that asshole, Hall, and his little punk sidekick, so we circled the back streets of the glitzy Gold Coast to get to Eddie's condo.

Neither Malik nor I were Chicago natives. We had to keep reminding each other of the directions and where we were at any given time. The important thing was to not run across Detective Hall again. We didn't.

We pulled into a dark alley two blocks from Eddie's. The truck crept along, at five miles an hour, with the headlights off until Malik found a spot to hide. He parked and we ran to Eddie's back entrance. The doorbell startled them inside.

"My God, I hope it's them," said Indigo as she sprinted to the door after squeezing Shalamar's hand for support.

Eddie cautiously led the way. "Listen, everybody. We're in big trouble here. Calm down and let's think about this for a minute. We don't know who's out there. If we go to that door, and it's not them, we might be asking for more trouble."

I could understand Eddie's reluctance; hell to be honest,

under the circumstances, I don't know if I would have opened the door either! But, Eddie did. If they had been wrong, and it wasn't us at the door, they would've been the ones in danger. After all, the past twenty-four hours had been full of threatening phone calls, attempted murder, and domestic violence.

"Who's there," asked Eddie in a trembling voice that he tried masking with added bass.

"It's me," I answered, hoping he would recognize my low voice.

"It's Jake!" Eddie gave reassurance to the others.

I could hear the whispering of cheers, the relieved gasps and the restrained handclaps through the door's intercom.

"Thank God," praised Indigo. "Thank You. Let them in, Eddie."

"What if it's a trick?" Eddie was overly cautious.

"Trick my ass," Indigo said. She wasn't one to use profanities. "You'd better push that damn button and let them in!"

"Go ahead, Eddie," Charlotte said, "before something else happens to them."

Eddie extended his long manicured finger. The buzz was loud and lasted for what seemed like a steady minute before the latch dropped and the door flung open. Indigo ran to me with Nicole right behind her looking for Malik. She grabbed him around the neck and jumped to wrap her legs around him.

When our reception came to an end, I hurried everyone inside. There, I encouraged them to be seated. I then began explaining all the dynamics of the whole affair. I started with my life after the divorce with Indigo. During that time, I knew I needed to improve a lot of things about myself in order to be successful in any relationship. The first few things that came to mind were my insensitivity, womanizing, bullshitting and irresponsible ways.

While I was in the midst of my self-discovery, rebounding from foolishness, I met Kayra. We had a good thing going for a while. A year into our relationship it all changed. Well, it wasn't our relationship that changed, it was me. Case in point. The night Malik and I got into a little spat, I should've known Jasmine's was the wrong place to go. It was the hottest nightclub in the city and full of temptation. Although it was not my intention, I messed up. Malik and I met Yolanda and her friend, Nicole. Malik made out on that deal. He found a soul mate, and I ended up getting busted by Kayra and Pam. They were guests of the club's manager that night and somehow, I allowed myself to get caught up in a compromising position with Yolanda.

Kayra was at the end of her rope with me, and the incident led to her placing me at the top of her long list of grievances with men. She ended our relationship and cut off all communication between us. Instead of acknowledging my stupidity, learning from it and moving on, I chose to make an attempt at redemption. A few days after the night at Jasmine's, I decided to trail Kayra in hopes of discovering if her rendezvous was with another man. This was based on her almost saying as much when she checked me in the club. Or so I thought it was a man, at the time. Little did I know Pam was a notorious undiscriminating Jezebel. She skillfully used her long friendship with Kayra to manipulate her, while she was at her weakest point. Pam seduced Kayra into a lesbian affair and encouraged her to continue to keep away from me forever.

When I followed Kayra that night, she was meeting with Pam. Not with some other stud, like I'd expected. I waited in my car a couple of blocks down the street from Pam's house. I only wanted to observe, but my pride got the best of me. I decided to go inside to stake my claim to Kayra. All of this, despite Malik's insistence on me not doing the obvious 'suicide mission.' He was especially reluctant about getting involved in the ordeal. He told me before he came, he wasn't taking any part in anything and the whole idea had disaster written all over it.

Malik sat and shook his head in agreement with my recollection of that infamous night. I continued with the story and told everyone how he stayed in the car, while I marched to the house. Inside, I searched for Kayra but she wasn't anywhere to be found. By this time, I knew something was definitely wrong. I wasn't aware of Kayra being trapped outside by some wild alley cat. I kept roaming about the house looking for her, while loud music blared from the bedroom. I followed the music anticipating Kayra to be there engulfed in passion. All I found was a ransacked room with no sign of Kayra or anyone else. I went into the master bedroom and there she was. An unidentified woman covered from head to toe in blood with her head nearly decapitated from her naked body. I approached closer to see if it was Kayra. It wasn't her. Then I bent over the body and in walked Kayra. She saw me and assumed she'd witnessed a murder, with me being the murderer! Kayra ran and called the police. I fled the scene. And within the next forty-eight hours, I was on a plane to Indigo's house in New York.

I stopped talking and looked around the room. Seated on the edge of the eggplant colored sofa were Charlotte, Vikki, Tarnisha, and Lawrence. To their right, on a matching love seat were Cedric and his wife, Karen, with Pops planted securely between them. Each sat with puzzled looks on their faces as they tried to keep up with all I'd said up to that point. Eddie stood, leaned up against the edge of the wet bar. His sculptured body loaded with large muscles tensed as his long arms folded. He appeared to be eagerly anticipating hearing more before he expressed whatever thoughts I saw there in his eyes.

For the first time all night, Tarnisha was quiet. She had taken the large studio chair as her own and was straddled across it with her long legs. Her short black hair was still silky from the wrap the stylist had done a few days before. It rested gently against her face covering her left eye. The other one focused on me. Indigo and Shalamar were far across the room on an animal printed sofa. Shalamar held Indigo's hand in a gesture of support. Her embarrassment was obvious. I guess she couldn't understand how I could be explaining my past indiscretions so openly in front of Indigo. The fact of the matter was, Indigo and I had discussed these things many times before.

Through our constant communication, prayer, strong love and hearts of forgiveness, we still managed to work our relationship out. But, she wasn't going to take any more nonsense from me. Shalamar was right in that sense. Indigo didn't like to be reminded of the things we both were trying so hard to forget.

* * *

I was able to convince myself that everybody had somehow begun understanding what all this had to do with each of them. If they didn't know, they'd better start figuring it out, I thought. I continued, reluctantly at first. There were still plenty of missing pieces and blanks left for me to fill in.

In New York, I went on, Indigo gave me thirty days to find the real killers and clear the whole thing up or leave. That was it. I was scared as hell of going to jail. Especially, over something I'd been falsely accused of doing. No matter what, I still needed Indigo and Railey's love. Each day that passed with them, I wanted their love even more. Then within two weeks,

Malik informed me the body found that night was not Kayra's friend, Pam. It was actually Pam's lover, Demetria Taylor, but the evidence pointed to Pam as being the real target.

Eventually, I was cleared. Two weeks later, Kayra was shot to death after another attempt on Pam's life. Subsequently, Pam suffered near fatal wounds in the incident. She recovered and then disappeared with the diary and the video, both belonging to Senator Morgan. After mentioning his name, everybody seemed to be awakened to the fact that this was not some ordinary shit we were in. I overlooked the dropped mouths and told them the diary and the video contained some sort of evidence that was embarrassing for the Senator. At the time, I didn't exactly know how much stuff was involved. Whatever it was, they were willing to kill over it. Our beloved Detective Hall, I explained, was the lead investigator of Demetria's murder. He had been the one to find evidence proving someone else committed the murders. Not me!

By now, Eddie and the others should have gotten it. The only reason I was cleared was because Detective Hall and his people, who worked for the Senator were the real killers. They needed me free because I'm sure they believed I'd lead them to Pam. And now three years later, the saga continued.

It was now coming to a head. I'm sure there was more to the story and to Pam's life than I shared, but that was everything I knew at the time. There was nothing else to say. The only thing left to do was to find the stuff and pray we could come up with a way of keeping them from killing again. Since none of us knew where to go or what to do, we said the hell with the hotel rooms and stayed at Eddie's house. There was safety in numbers, at least we hoped.

* * *

Morning came fast. Very fast. It was almost six in the morning and I was the first to get up. The sun was beginning to peep through the bluish-gray clouds. Dawn's light was brilliant with vivid orange streaks reflecting from the sky. I glanced over to Indigo who looked peaceful. At least, as peaceful as one could possibly be under the circumstances. Then I eased out of the king size bed we slept in inside one of Eddie's extra bedrooms and tried not to wake her. I peeped around the doorway and looked down the hall where I could see Cedric draped across the sofa. My eyes moved further, I saw Karen lying across him. She was half-dressed, in one of Eddie's big tee-shirts and her panties. They held each other tightly like they'd spent the night in fear.

Quietly, I tipped towards the other bedroom after stepping over Tarnisha and Shalamar, who were both knocked out on the floor. The rest were scattered about wherever they found a free place to crash.

I decided to go for a walk and smoke a cigar, even though they were a bit harsh for my taste. I wanted one anyway, so I walked towards the balcony holding up my pants unbuckled with one hand. When I reached for the cigars inside a humidor sitting on a table near the window ledge, I heard a car speeding around the corner down below. We were on the fifth floor, but the sounds of the city were still very much clear and traffic was not uncommon to hear.

Looking out of the window, I saw a black sedan pull up in front of the building. A short, stocky man wearing a dark suit and a wide brim hat got out of the car. In his arms was a brown package. He quickly walked to the entrance of the building where the doorman greeted him. They spoke briefly and the man gave the package to the doorman along with an envelope with what I assume was money inside. The doorman secured the package under his arms and put the envelope inside his pocket. The man hurried back to the car and sped away. Moments later, the doorbell rang and I ran to answer it. Through the door, a doorman identified himself. I looked through the peephole and recognized the youthful middle-aged man. Luckily, no one else heard a thing. I wanted to be the first to see what was going on with this early morning visit. I cracked the door only enough to see the package.

"Sir, I have a delivery for a Jake Alexander."

"That's me. Who is this from?"

"There was no information left by the sender. My boss just said to get this up here in a hurry."

"Fine! Just give it to me. Where do I sign?"

"Here, sir."

"There you go. Thank you."

I didn't even attempt to give him a tip or even a second look as I quietly closed the door shut. All I wanted was the package. I ran into the kitchen, then placed the mysterious delivery on the countertop and resisted tearing into it. Instead, I used a knife to cut open the brown wrapping to avoid making a noise, which might have alerted the others to what was happening.

Inside the box were manila folders with each of our names printed on them. On top was mine. Before I opened it, my hands shook uncontrollably. Why, exactly, was beyond me. Probably it was a combination of fear, curiosity, and stupidity for even being in the situation in the first place.

My nerves finally let up enough and allowed me the use of my body again. I opened the folder and looked around once again to ensure everyone was still asleep. They were. So, I read the first page of the document.

*Jake Bernard Alexander. Born 4 September 1962 in Austin, Texas. Raised in a three family home by both parents, Ruthy Mae Hudson and David Alexander. Average high school student who skipped classes and smoked plenty of marijuana. Attended a small college in southwest Texas. Has major problems with...*

There was more, but I didn't know if I wanted to see it. I thought to myself the preliminary information was no big deal. Anyone could have gotten the data, if they had half of a brain and knew how to access public records, well except the getting high part. However, when I turned the first page to read the second, I quickly realized what I was looking at wasn't just a typical biography of my life. I froze with anticipation of the next sentence. Then out of nowhere, I was interrupted.

"Jake, is that you," asked a quiet voice from the room nearby.

"Yeah, it's me," I whispered back. It was Eddie creeping in from the back.

"What are you doing?"

Eddie was easing himself down the hall, using the wall to support his strong athletic body. He wore a blue pair of Texas University shorts, which showed his long bowed legs, and a white T-shirt exposing broad shoulders.

"I'm not doing anything!"

"You're shittin' me, Jake. What are those?"

"Nothing. Just some folders I found."

"Nothing? Where did they come from? You're up this early with this 'I'm busted' look on your face. So, you can quit the crap and tell me what you're doing."

"You're right, Eddie."

"I know! So come clean."

"Damn! Come here, man. Let me show you this stuff."

"All right, what you got?"

"First take another look out there and make sure

everybody is still sleeping."

"Why?"

"I don't want anybody to see these right now. Not until I've had a chance to look at them."

"What's going on, boyfriend? You're scaring me."

"I'll tell you. Just take a look around."

"I'll be right back," assured Eddie.

"Hurry then, boyfriend!" joked Jake.

"Very funny. Be ready to explain when I get back." he replied.

"Yep." I said.

# Naked 5

"Is my wife going to be okay, Doctor?"

"Yes, Mr. Harris. She's going to be fine."

"Thank God!"

"Certainly. However, also be thankful the vase wasn't a few ounces heavier. If so, Mr. Harris, we might be having a much different conversation."

"How so, Doc?"

"Well, she could have sustained brain damage, skull fractures or faced a list of many other possible complications. Even death, Mr. Harris. She was very lucky."

"Damn! Are you trying to tell me my wife was almost killed?"

"Well..."

"Never mind, Doc."

"Those other things are not a concern. Your wife was

treated for a pretty deep laceration. We closed the wound with some stitches and she's going to be fine."

"Good!"

"Now, there is quite a bit of swelling, and she is going to experience considerable discomfort for the next few weeks. I've prescribed Percocets to help the pain. The swelling can be decreased by applying an ice-pack, three to four times a day. Make sure she follows my instructions."

"I can handle it, Doc."

"Any other questions, Mr. Harris?"

"When can I see her and how long before she can leave?"

"You can see her now, if you like. But, we'd like to keep her overnight for observation."

"All right, Doc. That will be fine. Where is she?"

"Come this way, Mr. Harris."

"Oh, Doc? By the way, my wife didn't mention how all of this happened, did she?"

"No. She wasn't able to go into any details. Our focus has been on her medical condition."

"And?"

"And, any other concerns you might have should be taken up with your wife and the authorities if necessary."

\* \* \*

"Hi, baby! How are you?"

"What! How am I? How in the hell do you think I'm feeling? Ouch. You wait. You just wait 'til I'm able to get out of this damn bed!"

"Baby."

"Baby, my ass."

"Sweetheart, please."

"Shut up!"

"Please, baby. Let's not get into that right now. I'm sorry for everything, but…"

"You're a sorry muthafucka, all right. I'm gonna' show you how sorry you really are after I beat yo' ass!"

"Sweetheart. Baby. Please. Just rest right now."

"I'm gone rest my foot in yo' ass!"

"I know I've got a lot of explaining to do. I…"

"Please! I don't want to hear it! Get the hell out of here! You make me sick!"

"Rachel? Baby?"

"Get out, you bastard!"

"Just give me a chance to…"

"Ooh. Just let me get up. I'll kick…ouch!"

"Here. Let me fix your pillow."

"Muthafucka, you get away from…ouch. Ooh."

"Wait."

"Wait?"

"Yes."

"Wait for what? For you to go out and fuck some other goddamn bitch?"

"No! Baby…"

"You probably already have. You just wait. Ouch. Get out!"

"Are you sure you want me to leave? Is there anything I can get you?"

"You can get the hell out of here! What part of G-E-T O-U-T, ouch, don't you understand? Nurse! Nurse!"

"Stop, baby! You don't have to do this."

"Get out! Nurse! Nurse!"

The door to the room flew open and a stern looking woman in her late fifties steps in with a hurried look on her face.

"Hey! Hey! What's going on in here?"

"Nurse, I want him out of here. Now!"

"Sir, I'm going to have to ask you to leave."

"Wait…"

"Now, sir!"

"Okay. Damn, let go of my arm."

"Look, sir. You're upsetting the patient."

"The patient? That's my wife!"

"Sir, this is the last time I'm asking you to leave. Otherwise, you will force me to call security."

"Get out! Arrest his ass!"

"Calm down, Mrs. Harris."

"Get his cheating ass out of here!"

"Sir..."

The nurse marched toward the phone to make good on her promise to get security involved.

"I'm going. Okay? Baby, I'll come back later when you're feeling better. Maybe then, we can talk about this."

"Kiss my ass!"

# Naked 6

"Everybody is still sleep. So, I'm listening. What's all this about, Jake?"

"Okay. This is the deal. I looked out of the window this morning, and some strange guy with a patch over his eye had that box of envelopes under his arms. Before I knew it, the doorman was ringing the doorbell with instructions from the doorman to bring the package up here."

"That's strange."

"I know."

"Did he say who it was from?"

"No."

"What did he say?"

"He didn't say anything. He just gave it to me and asked me to sign for it."

"Anyway, what are these?"

"These are what were in the package. I started looking at them when you came."

"And?"

"And, look at this."

"What?"

"Here."

"Damn! From the look of these documents, all this stuff is about each of you."

"I know."

"I don't see my name."

"Read the first one."

"This is for Malik."

"Whew! Well, go ahead and open it up."

"Are you sure?"

"Yeah."

"All right. Let's see what it says."

Eddie slowly pulled the folder from the small stack and carefully placed the rest back on top of the remaining ones. He held the folder gently, like a mother with her newborn gift. I assumed his delicate way was a direct offshoot of Eddie's newfound sensitivity. I knew that was probably an unfair assessment. But, oh well. At any rate, with our paranoia almost at its peak, we took a final glance behind us to make sure the coast was clear. Eddie began to read in a soft whisper.

*Malik Kalot. Born June 9, 1969, Shreveport, Louisiana. The oldest of three children born to Maribella Townsend and Minkemba Paige upon their naturalization from the Bahamas. After a brief marriage, the father was arrested for robbery, which included the shooting deaths of two policemen. The incident resulted in a life sentence for him in January 1978. Maribella remarried an autoworker named Lamar Woodard. This union shortly evolved into one of abuse and neglect. The mental torment became commonplace for Malik's mother, while sexual abuse was a regular occurrence for...*"

"Yeah, I got my ass beat!"

"Malik," I choked.

"Oops," blurted Eddie.

"What the hell is going on," Malik demanded.

"This," I quickly responded, handing over the answer in the form of the folder.

"What is it?"

Although he still seemed half-asleep, with squinted eyes and a hard early morning dick, his aggravation was obvious and warranted.

We were supposed to be friends. Here I was, behind Malik's back with somebody he didn't really know, reading the private secret kept within his soul for years. So painful and closely guarded, in fact, he hadn't even told me about it. Even with us being the closest of friends for many years, I knew the others would eventually find out. Therefore, now was as good a time as any to come clean.

"Where these come from?" He asked, settling down from his initial outrage, he still wanted some answers.

"Just read, man," I insisted. "Please, just read."

"You're not the only one," said Eddie. "Trust me."

I was sure he felt guilty about our apparent awkward predicament.

"You know what," asked Malik. "I'm not reading that shit."

"Look, man," I said. "I don't like it either. This stuff came this morning when I woke up. I'm almost certain it was Detective Hall and his crew that left it. He's probably going to try to blackmail us into finding that damn tape and diary."

"Shit!" Malik was obviously frustrated as he threw the folder back into the box, casting a dirty look at us. He sat on a nearby stool and his voice was broken as he fought through his tears. We could clearly sense his pain as he spoke."

"It started when I was about ten years old. Mama would go to work early in the morning. I can still remember her voice telling me to be a good boy and to mind while she was away. I hated to hear the door shut behind her. I knew when she left, it would just be him and me in that house. I believe he longed for the moment he'd have me to himself."

"Everyday, I cried and screamed for her to come back. 'Don't leave me, Mama,' I would beg. 'Please, Mama!' In her hastiness or just lack of sensitivity to my tears, she would bend down, breaking the sharp creases of her white hospital uniform and look me in the eyes. It was supposed to be a sincere attempt to convince me everything was going to be okay while she was gone. To this day, I don't know if Mama was just blindly in love or just blind."

"When her hand got done patting my head like some of puppy until I'd calm down. After which she would give me the same ol' script as before, then she stood up and ran through the door. I would cry even more. That muthafucker couldn't wait for the damn door to slam. I'd still be crying, praying for Mama to come back, when he'd begin yelling at me to shut up. The harder I tried to stop, the more I heard his raspy cigarette voice get louder. 'Shut the fuck up, you little bastard!' he'd shout. I tried hiding by running to my room and closing the door. But every time, he'd burst inside and yell more. 'Stop crying and git your ass up!'

"I can still smell the stench of cheap liquor and Marlboro cigarettes on that bastard's breath. I still remember the feeling of the sheets being snatched off of me and his cold, rough hand slapping my back. He grabbed me by my throat to stop me from crying until I couldn't fuckin' breathe anymore. Just before I'd pass out, he'd throw me onto the bed."

"The punches came hard to my stomach and chest. Anywhere the muthafucker could find that wouldn't show bruises. 'Stop! Stop!' I'd cry after every blow. He wouldn't even pause. Matter of fact, they'd get harder. Soon after that, he'd pulled my pajamas down and…"

"You don't have to tell us," I said to Malik.

"No, I need to," he answered.

"I don't know if I want him to," Eddie said.

"Are you okay?" I asked him.

"Yeah."

Malik broke into tears. For the first time he'd opened up his private Pandora's Box of pain and buried secrets. Eddie and I became hard-pressed to hold back droplets of our own when he started again.

"Don't!" I'd yell. The bastard wouldn't listen. He just pull my pajamas down to my ankles. Then grab my…my…and spread my legs apart. He was so heavy, I couldn't even move. I mean, I was just a child and he stuck it in me like I was, was nothing. A lifeless doll or something. Sometimes he'd be nice enough to use Vaseline, like he was doing me a fuckin' favor. When does getting raped become a pleasure? It don't!"

"Man, I didn't know." I said. "You're like the only brother I've known."

"I know you didn't know, because I never planned on telling you," he said. "What was I supposed to say? Blurt out and say, 'Hey! Guess what, Jake? As a kid, I took it up the ass by my sick ass stepfather!' My intentions were to try and forget. Mama was fuckin' clueless. She couldn't see around his bullshit, sweet talk and empty promises. Or she just didn't want to see. That fucker never even had a damn job-at least not a legal one. At one time he claimed to be in the car business, but actually he ran numbers. Mama pretended everything was just great, going along with the loving husband and wife routine. I should have known how wide open Mama's nose was over him. I never even bothered to tell her about what happened. Well, that's not entirely true." Malik paused and turned his attention to me.

"I...I...need some cold water. Get me something to drink please."

"Here," I offered. "Drink this."

"Whew," exclaimed Malik. "Thanks. I get cotton mouth whenever I start thinking about this shit."

He continued. Eddie and I kept quiet.

"I guess I didn't want to hurt her. I blamed my limp and soreness on falls at school. I made it up. Just like that. I was nine at the time."

"After the first time, I hated him. And I hated her because if she loved me like she said she did, I thought, she wouldn't have left me at home with the son-of-a-bitch! I hated her for it. When I started getting a little older, maybe twelve, he eventually stopped. That only made matters worse."

"The first time I saw him punch her was when I was in either the sixth or seventh grade. He came in yelling about how some bookie didn't come through on some winnings or something like that. This of course, after spending the whole night out. He fussed about how Mama didn't have his breakfast ready and how she was not looking like she used to."

"After going into their room to take off his shoes, he heard Mama and me laughing in the kitchen. It was the first time in over two years we'd sat and had fun with each other. A mother bonding with her son, you know? She even actually looked me in the eyes and managed to convince me that she did give a damn. It was at that very moment I almost told her what had been going on, while she was gone, helping clean the asses of all those old white bastards at the hospital."

"Before I could get the first words out, this crazy mutha-fucka comes running his ass in there yelling. For some reason, he thought we were talking about him. He must have felt guilty for the shit he'd been doing."

"This time Mama didn't listen to him. She told him she was talking to her son and he had no right to trip about it. The final straw came when she screamed he didn't have a real job anyway and the last thing he should be worried worry about was our early morning conversation disturbing him. He snapped right then, grabbed Mama's favorite plate and smashed it across her face, knocking out her two front teeth. Then he put his hands around her neck and choked her. Man, I lost it. I ran and kicked the shit out of him, right in the balls. The punk lifted his hand and swung a fierce backhand slap that landed me against the wall, knocking me out cold. My eye stayed swollen shut for a week. After that, he made me stay locked up in the room so nobody at school would find out what had happened."

"Two weeks later, he and Mama fought again. I was hit again. It wasn't until the following year, after God only knows how many more beatdowns, Mama finally realized the fucker was crazy and she had to get away from his ass before he killed us!"

"Well, by this time, he'd gotten a job stocking shelves at a local grocery store. He was going to change his ways, he told Mama. He said he was going to lighten up on us a bit. Whatever the hell that meant! Like he was doing us a damn favor by kicking our asses two times a week instead of seven! Mama wasn't even trying to hear it now. She'd made up her mind we were leaving. Boy, did we try!"

* * *

Now I was even more engulfed. This was serious shit! Malik told it like he was some kind of campfire storyteller and we were roasting marshmallows over his life's travails. After twenty years of friendship with Malik, it was as if I didn't know a single thing about him anymore. This looming array of a shit load of unanswered questions hovered in the air, suffocating Eddie and me. Either this dude was lying his ass off, or I just wasn't getting it. Whichever it was, Malik continued with all the vivid details.

"July 7th, 1982, three days after Independence Day. I'll

never forget it. Mama must've felt freedom in the air. We'd gotten back from Big Mama's house down south for the annual family reunion barbecue. All three of us were exhausted from the long drive, which seemed like it would never end. I was in bed asleep before the car engine even cooled off. Him and mama weren't far behind me, except soon after they got in and dropped their bags, they were doing their thing in the bedroom. He was sexin' mama so hard the headboard kept banging against the wall waking me up. The bumping eventually stopped. A few hours later, mama sneaked into my room, snatched the covers off of me, and whispered, 'Get up! Get up, we're leaving'

I asked, 'Where we goin', mama?'

"Mama don't know just yet, baby,' she said, her two false front teeth just as white as the others. 'But we're getting out of here. Be real quiet. Come on, we got to put your clothes on. Come here!"

"I'm scared."

'I know, baby. Don't you want mama to take us away from here?'

"Yeah."

'Look at me. Don't turn away, baby. I know this hasn't been easy for you. Mama knows she should've paid more atten-tion to her unhappy little man. I'm sorry. Oh, baby, I'm so sorry for everything, Sugah.'

"It's okay, mama. Please don't cry. Let's go, I'm ready."

'Everything will be okay.'

"I love you, too, Mama. Mama?"

'Yes, baby?'

"I...I need to tell you something. It's about Lamar."

'What is it, baby?'

"He's been..."

'Hush, tell me later. I heard him stirring around in there. We've got to go!'

# N a k e d  7

The drive from the hospital was slow and quiet. Ray found himself dazed with guilt for allowing the wheels to fall off of his love wagon. Palms sweating, he thought...Play-a! Play-a! Busted! The woman he loved and had promised a lifetime of faithfulness. The woman he'd lied to and lusted after. Both gone. Rachel's anger and disappointment had already been expressed. That was only half of the story. How Ray would handle Shalamar, was the other.

He hoped she'd get everything out of her system. He'd apologize for being a lying, low down, insensitive and stupid ass man. Then they both could go their separate ways. Far away. When everything died down and the smoke cleared, maybe he could reconcile with his wife. Only if she could muster up enough forgiveness in her heart to take him back. It was a long shot, indeed, but it had been done before. I knew this to be true from my own humbling experience. Though, from what I knew of Rachel, Ray's task would be difficult at best. Nevertheless, Ray's cheating ass had the problem. We were attempting to save our lives! Ray's situation was just more bullshit the rest of us didn't need.

\* \* \*

Ray sped through town like a bat out of hell. His stop at the local tavern was effortless and spontaneous. When he saw the blue fluorescent lights of the club, they called his name in a titillating manner. The way that a seductress would lure a loyal and faithful husband. Before he knew it, Ray found himself parked and sitting on an empty stool at the bar ordering a drink. Cautiously, he dispensed his guilty conscious into a tall shot of Tequila. 1800. Black Label.

When he swallowed the first shot and slammed it down his throat, it burned like hell. Soon it simmered to just a tingle. After the next two shots, the numbness settled in and the grimace on his face which was once so defined, became closer to a smile. The liquor began to caress him from the inside out as it went down.

"Give me another," said Ray. "Matter of fact, make this one a double."

"You look like a man with a lot on his mind," the short, fat bartender with the missing finger said. "Drinking like one, too!"

"Well, I am glad you're so fuckin' observant, my dear man," slurred Ray. "I...I...just might have a thing or two that I...uh...need to toss over the bridge."

"Ain't but two things that'll make a man drink like that."

"Is that right?"

"Yep!"

"Should I even bother to ask?"

"Sure. Why not?"

"Okay. Spit it out. No, don't! Shit! What would you know about my problems?"

"You'd be surprised."

"Whatever. The two things?"

"Hmmm...let me see. From the look of the face on that watch, I would say maybe Rolex, money is probably not the problem. Unless of course, you recently ran into some gambling troubles. But, you're too smart for that. No, I definitely sense a woman problem here. Hell, you can be a genius and still be reduced to a head of lettuce when it comes to them."

"Okay. Okay. You're right."

"Son, you didn't even need to bother. Let me guess. It's your wife?"

"I didn't say I was married."

"You didn't have to. The ring gave it away."

"Oh."

"Want to tell me about it?"

"No."

"Suit yourself. I'll be right back with that drink."

"How about that! So you do, do more than practice cheap ass psycho therapy?"

"Here you go, sir. Make this your last cocktail for a while. Go cool off and sober up. No need to compound your problems with trouble from the law. No cheap ass psycho therapy intended."

"You got jokes, too, I see. What's your name, by the way?"

"Maynard. Yours?"

"Raymond. Call me Ray-Ray."

"Okay, Ray-Ray. Pleased to meet you."

"Yeah man, me too. You were right you know?"

"About?"

"My problem."

"Oh, we're back to that again? Hmm...I see. Well, like you said, your problem is your problem."

"So, you're not talking to me about it now?"

"Hey, I just thought you needed an ear. That's usually part of my job. To listen. Okay, maybe I give a little advice, too-if it's asked for or I think it's necessary."

"Guess my problem must've spelled n-e-c-e-s-s-a-r-y, 'cause I don't remember asking."

"You don't get it, do you, son? It's not always what you

say that counts. That's my gift; I can read people."

"Look, Mayonnaise. I'm drunk and I got problems. Right about now, it's a little difficult to be receptive to your obvious many talents."

"Is that why you're afraid of me?"

"Afraid of you?"

"Yeah, afraid. Ain't you? Look into the deepest part of your soul and tell me you're not."

"I've told you. I'm not. What do you want from me?"

"Look, Ray. Let's get it straight. I'm not looking for anything from you. But, you do need me."

"For?"

"Your soul. I'm here to clear your conscience and free your soul. Repent, Ray! Repent now before it's too late."

"What?"

"Tell me about what you did. Your wife, Ray. Tell me what you did to her. Have you caused her pain?

"I did. Look, man. I don't know who or what you are, but I did. I hurt her bad. She...uhh...she found out about an affair I had with another woman. And because of what I did, she's in the hospital. There, you have it! Happy now?"

"How do you feel about what you did?"

"Like shit. At the time, it filled a void. I told my wife what I was missing. Rachel claimed she wasn't the affectionate type anymore. Hell, we've only been married for a couple of years. What the fuck? Things shouldn't change like that. Not in two years! I'm sorry. I was wrong. Very wrong."

"What have you learned?"

"Never to betray those I love. My God and my wife being at the top of that list."

"I see. Do you seek forgiveness?"

"I do."

"Ask him and turn away from the evil that has gotten you to this point."

"I will."

"Just think about what I'm saying. Now is *not* the time for your deep contemplation over spiritual matters. You've been drinking heavily and the words I share are for your soul. Therefore, they must be fully digested by the mind, body and spirit in clear conscience."

"I feel you. I'll be praying about that, definitely. Thanks for knowing what buttons to push. I'm still confused about you. There must be another side. What else do you do? I know you're not just a bartender, are you?"

"That's an interesting question. What do you believe I am, Raymond?"

"I don't know. Maybe, some kind of spiritual guru or something? You tell me."

"I told you before that you needed me. Either way, you're free! Free to move from the evil of your wicked ways, or free to remain locked in them. Do you remember what you told me?"

"Never to betray the ones I love?"

"Will you commit to that?"

"It's either that or feel the way I do now. And, I don't want that. I don't want to lose my wife. Damn it! I don't want to lose her."

"I have a feeling that you won't. At least, not this time, Raymond, if you do as you say and ask for forgiveness. Be honest with your wife once the appropriate time comes and you two are able to communicate again without the anger and pain."

"You think I still have a chance?"

"Trust me. Just keep my words in your heart. Let not the moment of tonight be in vain. Do you understand, Raymond?"

"Yeah, I do believe."

"The gates opened with the words you spoke. Believe. Just believe."

"I do."

"Enough said for now. Why don't you call someone to come and get you? It's been a long night and tequila doesn't let up easy, you know what I mean?"

"What? I look drunk to you?"

"No, not if you can ask me that again with your eyes opened."

"Whew! You got me on that one. I'll be right back.

Where are the phones?"

"Right over there, near the pool tables."

Raymond carefully monitored each step he took. He maneuvered his way through the crowded club and the mob of people gathered around the pool tables.

"Oops, excuse me. Excuse me. Excuse me...coming through over here."

"Ooh, hey, sexy," purred a vivacious looking vixen dressed in a short powdered blue skirt and tall heels that accentuated her long legs.

"Hello and good-bye," replied Ray rudely.

"What's wrong, sweetie? You can't just bump a girl with those strong shoulders and then just walk away."

"Oh, believe me. I can!"

"That's too bad."

"I'm sure it is. I'm sure it is. Excuse me. Coming through. There it is, finally. The phone."

Ray picked up the grubby receiver and wiped it down with the free end of his shirt.

"Okay," thought Ray. "Now, what is Eddie's number? It's in my data bank, which I don't have. Damn! Okay. Okay. Let me think. Eddie. Eddie. I know, I know it. It's...let's see...7...no 9-4-1...no...9-4-3. Let me think...943-82. No, damn it! I must be drunk. Okay, 9-4-3...9-4-3-8-2-6-1. I'll dial that one. Here we go. Oh, I got to put change in this damn thing. Change.

Change. Do I have change? Here we go, a quarter and a dime. Take this you muthafucka."

"Hello. Ed's Catfish House."

"Ed?"

"Yeah, this is Ed."

"This is Ray. Come and get me. I'm at some bar on 78th and Halsted."

"Son, who are you? This is Ed's Catfish House. I'm Ed and this is my place of business. Who you after boy? I don't know a Ray."

"Wait a minute. You're not my Eddie. Damn! Wrong number! What was it again? 9-4-3-8-2-6-1. Okay. If this doesn't work, I'll just spend the night here. Here goes nothing. 9-4-3-2-8-1-6."

"Hello."

"This is Raymond. Who's this?"

"Ray, where the hell are you," I asked. "It's four o'clock in the damn morning. You're trippin' man."

"I'm at some tavern on 78th and Halsted. I need a ride. Been drinking a while, and I'm a little drunk."

"A little?"

"Okay, I'm drunk. There! Now, can you come and get me?"

"Here's Eddie. Don't you go anywhere. And, please, Ray, don't do anything stupid, okay?"

"You have my word."

"Ray," said Eddie talking into the phone, "where are you? How are you? And where's my...?"

"I'm cool, and the car is right here, outside. I don't know the name of this joint. Hold on. Hey! Hey! What's this place called?"

"What?" sounded the raspy voice of a tall well-dressed elderly man, who looked anxious to get his groove on.

"What's the name of this place?"

"*The Blue Bird*," the man answered.

"*The Blue Bird?*"

"Yeah," he answered again. "*The Blue Bird*."

"Heard of *The Blue Bird*, Eddie?"

" What?! How in the world did you find your way to *The Blue Bird?*" Eddie asked astonished. "I guess that explains why you're drunk this time of morning. *The Bird* will do it every time. I guess you found out what goes on in there."

"Hell yeah! I found that out as soon as I got in here. Anyway, I needed a drink. I went to see Rachel and she wasn't having it, hearing it, and was like fuck it!"

"Can you blame her? Don't answer that. I'll be right there. Give me about thirty minutes."

"Cool. I'll be at the bar."

"Please. That's why I have to come and get you in the first place. Just make sure you stay your ass out of my car. First my truck gets shot at, and now you're out drunk in my damn car."

"What you talking about? Shot at? What? What happened?"

"I'll tell you when I see you. With friends like y'all...never mind. I'm on my way."

"See you when you get here. Peace out."

Ray shuffled his way back through the crowd until the bar again became visible.

"Hmm. I don't see Maynard. Wonder where he went off to? Maybe he stepped away for a few minutes. He'll probably be back by the time I make it up to the bar. That's if I can ever make it through this crowded ass place. Excuse me. Excuse me."

"Hi, it's you again, sweetie," said the vixen from earlier in the evening. "Still haven't found who you're looking for?"

"I don't believe it. It's you again."

"It's me, baby! Changed your mind yet?"

"Girl, I already told you, I can't be fooling with you."

"Well, sweetie, too bad we won't be getting better acquainted."

"Yeah, my loss. Gotta' go! Excuse me. Excuse me."

"Aw!"

Ray approached the bar counter to find the bartender who'd counseled him gone, in his stead was a tall thin guy with very bad breath and who kept a permanent frown attached to his face.

"There you go, sir," the bartender said, finishing up with his customer. "Rum and coke with a twist of orange." He then turned his attention to Ray.

"What can I get for you, buddy?"

A quizzical look came over Ray's face, as he noticed the stranger now in Maynard's place.

"Hmm...nothing, I guess. I...I...don't want anything. Where is Maynard?"

"Maynard? Don't know him."

"You know," pressed Ray. "Maynard. The bartender in this spot earlier. Short. Stocky guy."

"Nobody working here like that."

"Come on! You've got to be kidding me! I was just here talking to him no more than twenty minutes ago."

"Sorry, Pal. I've been working at *The Bird* for five years. Never heard of...of...who was it? Maverick?"

"Maynard. He was here!"

"Look, buddy! Ain't no Maynard or Maverick, whoever, working behind my bar. Now can I get you something to drink? Might help with that bad memory of yours."

"I don't want another...see? Maynard wouldn't have let me have another... Oh, never mind."

"Ralph. Come here."

"Yeah, Willie? What is it?"

"Buddy, this is Ralph. Ralph, here, is the bartender who serves that end of the bar. Ralph, have you seen a short, stocky fellow named Maynard behind here?"

"Yeah, he had a missing finger," added Ray.

"What?" asked Ralph.

"Buddy here..."

"It's Ray."

"Ray, here" replied Willie sarcastically, "seems to believe there was some other bartender here at my station serving him. He says a short, stocky guy named, Mavis or something."

"Maynard!" corrected Ray.

"Okay, Maynard. Heard of him?

"Nobody I know of," said Ralph. "Far as I know, you and me are the only ones here tonight. Hey, you look familiar. What's your name again?"

"Ray."

"You've been here long?"

"Yeah. That's what I've been trying to tell you two idiots. I've been here drinking for the past two hours or so. And guess who got me drunk?"

"Ray!" It was a familiar voice just a few feet behind him. "Time to go."

"Eddie?"

"It's me."

"What's up, man?"

"You still trying to drink?"

"No. I was trying to get Maynard to come back."

"Who's Maynard?"

"Hey, big guy," said Willie to Eddie. "Is this your friend?

"I guess you could say that. I came to pick his ass up before he got into more trouble."

"Just checking. Looks like he's had a few. Buddy here has been asking about some mystery man, named Maynard. Ever heard of him?"

"Not at all."

"Us either. Take him home and let him sleep it off. Unless, maybe, he's looking for a new boyfriend. Hey, Ray? You play for the other team? Ralph, what do you think?"

"I think Ray got the hots for Mr. Maynard. He must have bought him a few drinks and whispered sweet nothings in his ear."

"Fuck both of you," Ray said, pissed off. "I know who I saw and where I saw him at."

"For the last time, your boyfriend doesn't work back here. I'm sure there are lots of other switch hitters around *The Bird* who can make your toes curl."

"I'm not a faggot!"

"No, that would be me!" sounded Eddie firmly.

"Now, let's go, Ray."

"Eddie, I didn't mean it that way. I wasn't trying to..."

"Never mind trying to convince me. I really don't care much about who or what you're fucking, nor whatever your thoughts are about me!"

# Naked 8

The last thing we wanted to do was open another folder. But they kept calling us. Daring us to open them, enticing everyone like a bad habit we were trying to quit. We fell for it like a two-dollar whore offered three dollars for a trick.

"You okay," I asked. "I don't know what to say. I really don't."

"There ain't nothing to say," Malik replied. "My life is on a damn stage, and I don't know what to do about it. I had forgotten about that shit in my life. At least, I tried to. It's been hard at times. For the most part, I put it out of my mind. In those late hours of the night when it's quiet, I..., I just...forget it."

"You don't have to tell me anything, Malik," I insisted.

"It's okay," he said. "That's only half the story. Look.

There's something that I think you should know. No. It's something that you need to know."

"What are you talking about," I asked. "What is it?" There was already enough drama. We didn't need more.

"Ask me. Go ahead and ask me what happened to him," insisted Malik.

"Okay," I said. "What happened to him?"

"He's dead. I killed his ass!"

"Oh shit! Damn! You're not serious are you? You've got to be kidding, right? Right? Malik?"

"I ain't fucking kiddin', Jake," he said, looking me dead in the eyes. "Damn straight, I did. That muthafucka got what the hell he deserved. I'd do it again if I could."

"Stop," I told Malik. "Just stop it, man. You're upset right now."

"What! You don't believe me?"

"Let me get this right. You're trying to tell me you killed your stepfather?"

"I don't know how to say it any plainer!"

"I can't believe we're having this conversation."

"Fuck you!" he said. "We're having this conversation because of the bullshit you did! Shit that you did. Not me. Remember: Kayra is how all of this shit got started in the first place. If you wouldn't been poking your damn dick where it didn't belong, there wouldn't have been a murder, or at least not one with all of us in the middle of it. Most of all, there wouldn't be these damn folders!"

"You trying to blame me? You must be out of yo' mind! You're the one who's talking about killing somebody!"

"This is way beyond what you think. You don't even have a fucking clue about what this shit has been doing to me since I was a kid. My life is not what it was. I'm not who I was. So, before either of you pass judgement my way, I'm getting the fuck out of here. Right now!"

"Wait!" I said. "Just wait a minute."

"Wait for what? Some more shit to come up popping up outta' of nowhere? I hope Kayra's pussy was worth all of this."

"Man, Kayra's dead. There's nothing anybody can do about it. I can't go back and change things. Who knew this stuff would come up about you?"

"Come up my ass, Jake! Never mind. Whatever!"

* * *

I pulled the box from underneath the table where I'd thrown it when we'd heard footsteps coming. I slammed it on the counter, ripped the lid off and revealed the rest of the folders. Malik still held his tightly in his hand. Then he lifted his head from the counter and turned to give us a 'kiss my ass' look we felt right down to the bone.

I ignored his furious eyes, or at least tried to as I reached in the box and lifted another folder. The name printed on the outside was Nicole's, Malik's wife. It was just our luck, as if he hadn't gone through enough in the past few minutes. Now, whatever might've been secretly stashed away in his wife's life was about to be exposed.

*Nicole Harrington. Born April 15, 1962. Her mother, Marie, was a one time Black Panther member sentenced to a seven-year prison term at an Arizona facility, where she bore a daughter named Nicole, while incarcerated. Eighteen years later, Nicole became a victim of a violent rape and bore a daughter of her own. Before the child's birth, she made a decision to give the baby away for adoption. Nicole stated, "To look into the baby's eyes would only be a constant reminder of how he came to be."*

"Stop," a voice screamed. "Stop! I don't want to hear anymore!" It was Nicole as she came into the kitchen trying to snatch away the folder. The words screeched from her lips, arms desperately grabbed for her life's story.

"That's not fair!" she cried. "It wasn't my fault! It wasn't my fault. A part of me died that day and each day I'm reminded of it. It wasn't my fault!"

Malik obviously hadn't been aware of his wife's ordeal by the way his mouth opened and those steel eyes beamed in her direction.

"Nicole!" he exclaimed. "What the hell! Why didn't you tell me?"

His words were slow. A reflection of the past two years

of their marriage came immediately to mind. It had been a beautiful union, but not without its fair share of problems and concerns. One of them, sexual. It was loving, passionate and most of the time, damn good! But, on occasion, Malik would sense a distance between them that interfered with their ability to make love on a regular basis. The headaches she claimed to have to avoid sex or the times that she just wasn't in the mood, became so many he could no longer keep count. The routine became the slow journey into the bathroom where he'd jerk off to magazines to fill his void. When he'd asked why she has so many headaches when the aspirin bottle was still unopened in the box, she never had an answer. But now, it all became crystal clear. It was all coming together and making sense because of the folders.

"I didn't know how to tell you," wept Nicole.

"But, I'm your husband. Didn't you think I would want to know?"

"Yes. I guess, I was just too scared I'd lose you."

"I'm your husband, Nicole! What were you thinking? What? I wouldn't have married you if you told me?"

"I don't know. Maybe."

* * *

I sympathized with Malik. He had a lot of explaining to do, himself, before he could be angry with Nicole. She hadn't been in the room when his stuff came out. Therefore, she was unaware of his little hidden secrets. I recalled a saying that seemed to fit the moment. 'Those who live in glass houses shouldn't throw stones.' I guess how Malik figured it; Nicole's situation caused unnecessary stresses in their relationship and affected their intimacy. On the other hand, one could argue Malik's own sexual abuse, as unfortunate as it was, was equally major in the sometimes distance he and his wife experienced. How I saw it, neither was to blame. Both of them suffered major trauma from sexual abuse. Now, each would have to confront the other in truth in order to save their marriage.

Malik began first, but was quickly interrupted by Nicole's readiness to finally free herself from the lingering night-mares crowding her mind, leaving her unable to completely give herself to her man.

"Wait a minute, darling," said Malik. "I want to explain first. I need to say something."

"Please, Malik," she asked. "Let me. I owe you that." We all moved into the living room and sat down then she began.

"It was a long time ago, although I've remembered it each day of my life since. I had just turned nineteen at the time. We'd come back to the dorms from a Spring concert held on campus. I don't remember what time it was, but it was definitely late. My three roommates, Barbara, Yolanda and Jody, along with three of Jody's guy friends. Everybody was in my room finishing up the liquor we'd bought before the concert.

Everything was all fun and games at first. After the drinks were gone and we were all drunk, it became much more than that. A lot more."

"Barbara and Jody went giggling out of the door, followed by two of the guys. Left in my room with me were Yolanda and the other guy that knew Jody. His name was Paul, and he was just along with the guys for the ride. From the moment I first saw him, I felt a cold streak run through me. He just seemed scary with those pale blue eyes. He was constantly forcing a smile when he looked at me. Yolanda's boyfriend had come in and before long, those two were out the door headed to his room, which I think was about three floors up. It seemed innocent, at first, when Paul asked to stay a little longer and talk. Plus, Yolanda didn't want me to follow her because she was about to get her 'itch' scratched."

"She and her boyfriend Steven, left while Paul remained in my room. I was nervous as hell, at first. But, we actually began having a good conversation. He told me how he was the captain on the school's football team. Of course, I didn't know a thing about ball playing."

"I got us some tea and turned on the TV. I began feeling his eyes on me a little too much, though. Soon, he had eased close enough to me where our thighs were actually touching each other's. Then he asked me for a kiss as he lifted my hand and placed it onto his groin. I thought he was kind of cute. Plus,

I'd never kissed a white guy before."

"What the fuck!" yelled Malik. "A fucking cracker did that shit to you? A fucking white boy raped you? I'll kill that muthafucka!"

"Let her finish, Malik," I said, interrupting his tirade.

"I said 'yes,'" she continued.

"And we kissed. It was nice. But, I immediately told him goodnight after he'd asked for another. He kept on insisting, telling me how he loved black women, how his family's maid was black, how he always dreamed of marrying Diana Ross. That shit actually began pissing me off instead of turning me on to him. I offered him a hug, instead. Then he just snapped and demanded another kiss. I got up and walked toward the door with him following closely behind. I tried pushing him out the door, but I felt his hand tighten around my arm, pulling me closer to him. He started...he started...rubbing his...his...thing in between my thighs. When I realized he wasn't going to stop, I screamed. 'Quit!' But he was forcing his lips all over mine. I spit dead in his eyes. That must've pissed him off because he shoved me to the ground and slammed the door shut."

"I screamed louder for help. Yolanda's room was three floors up and there was no telling where the others were. It was late Saturday night, and everybody was probably out partying or doing whatever, while I was alone with that mad man. The white bastard covered my mouth with one of his hands and started punching me with the other. My screaming stopped and I momentarily passed out. Even though I was half-conscious, I could still feel my shirt being ripped and my panties being pulled down from underneath my skirt. He opened my legs frantically and began forcing himself inside me. I came to and saw him staring at me, smiling. His blue eyes, like a devil's. When he saw my eyes open, he asked me how I liked it. How I liked being fucked by a real man, not a monkey-ass ape. Then, he turned me over so I couldn't see him. He forced it back inside me and pulled my hair until I thought my neck would snap. He grunted and kept asking me how I liked it, how I liked being fucked by a real man, as he pushed my head to the floor."

"When he was done with his business, he turned me over again. And he...he...he made me taste him. I swear I tried to bite that fucker's dick off! I managed to get out of the door while he was on the floor moaning and cursing me. I don't know how I did it, but I got to Steven's room. He and Yolanda heard me banging on the door crying for help. I had no clothes on. I was too busy crying and in shock to worry about being ashamed. They finally opened the door. She put a robe on me while Steven called security. A little while later, security found Paul laying on the floor, bleeding from the bite and the ass kicking Steven gave him before they got to the room."

"That's how it ended. Paul was handcuffed and rushed to the hospital. They arraigned him the next month. When his trial eventually came up, they sentenced him to only community service and placed him on probation. His rich family had hired some high-profile lawyers who convinced, the all-white jury, I had actually wanted it since I did initially kiss him."

"Fucking white boys can violate our women and not a damn thing happens," said Malik. "Let a brother even breathe hard on one of their cracker bitches, and we might not ever see the light of day again. Fuck that!"

"Leave it alone, man," I said.

"You say something?" he huffed at me. He looked like he was ready to throw punches at any second if I'd answered the wrong way.

"Nothing," I replied sharply, in an effort not to say more than I should and chance getting Malik further on the defensive. Kicking his ass now wouldn't help. I figured I'd use the energy elsewhere.

"And they bought that bull?" asked Indigo. Everyone was now awake.

"Girl, you know they wasn't gone let no white blue-eyed, ball player go to jail for raping a black woman," added Tarnisha.

"I hate those white muthafuckers," shouted Malik, who looked like he would explode if a pin dropped.

"It's okay, love," Nicole said to him.

"Where is that white son-of-a-bitch," demanded Malik.

"Is he still around? I'll kill his ass!"

"Baby, that was a long time ago," said Nicole. "He's probably moved away just as I have."

"Then, I'll find that punk," he said.

"Then what?" she asked. "Get yourself put in jail for life? Be another one of our beautiful brothers behind bars. No! I don't want that for my man, damn it!"

"You're right, girl," Indigo agreed.

"I don't like it!" Malik loudly yelled in response. "The shit ain't fair! When does it end?"

"It might not ever end," Nicole tried to reassure him. "Who knows the ways of white folks? One thing I do know, I will have my man."

"Yeah, you'll have me. Baby, you are one helluva' black woman."

"And you my dear, are one helluva' black man."

"Don't you ever forget it either."

"No, don't you forget it."

"Don't either of you forget the shit we're in," said Cedric, breaking up the Hallmark moment. "Sorry to be an asshole, but we need to concentrate on getting out of here alive."

"I know that's right," said T.J.

"Shit," said Kenny. "That's for damn sure. But, I'm sorry to hear about your tragedy."

"Yeah," I said. "Nicole, I'm sure Kenny and Cedric

aren't trying to be insensitive. I know I'm not. Malik, I love you, man. And, I do care."

"I know you care," he said.

"Good," I replied, happy to see that weight lifted from his shoulders. "I'm glad."

"Nicole," called Malik. "Come here, baby."

Her short steady walk to Malik was slow and purposeful. Nicole held him lovingly with the very essence of her soul. Malik gave of himself like he'd never before. Their embrace, even in the presence of us intruders in their lives, said what their words had been unable to.

Nicole's flowered dress, which doubled that night as a nightgown, crinkled from the tight way Malik held her. She matched his strength with her arms wrapped underneath his chest, filling her hands with his broad shoulders.

A peace covered the room, though it was just a temporary distraction from what was really going on with all of us. The morning seemed to be full of them. Everyone had become unraveled at the seams. Even I began wondering if we would destroy ourselves before Detective Hall even got a chance to! He was already damn near up our asses. There was no sense for us to make his job any easier.

Nicole and Malik were now situated. I, however, still remained cautious not to get the least bit comfortable. The next name on the folders was my own. Silently, I diverted the attention quickly to another folder, which I'd held in my right hand, while with my left, I eased my folder to the floor beside me. The name in the right hand read Yolanda Sanders. Now that was a name I hadn't heard in a while. Although she wasn't present, everyone including Indigo heard about our little bit of history---one that was connected directly to Kayra's death. Or should I say, Kayra's murder. Indigo knew Yolanda was a woman I'd been intimate with, if there were such a thing as intimacy with a one-night stand of straight freakin'! Either way, been there, done that, and the facts with all the sloppy details were, let's just say, an inside joke that wasn't funny. Kayra's murder was a byproduct of my involvement with Yolanda. My affair with her led to Kayra's and my breakup, which, in turn, led to Kayra's going to Pam's house the night that Detective Hall killed her by association. If I hadn't been so foolish to let my little head do the thinking for the big one, there wouldn't have been a Yolanda for Kayra to find out about. She more than likely wouldn't have confided her broken heart to Pam, while spending a deadly amount of time in her company.

That sneaky, lying, murderous bitch Pam Johnson was the seed that sprouted all of this. Where was she? I had to ask myself. Here I was trying to stabilize an out of control situation she alone was responsible for. Senator Morgan's beef was with her, not Yolanda or any of the rest of us for that matter.

I paused before saying Yolanda's name, although Indigo

was leaning over my shoulder and read the name as I closed the folder and slowly placed it back into the box. Indigo's eyes said what her lips didn't. I, in turn, glanced away with my eyebrows raised anticipating some sort of retaliation when I redirected the attention to Pam Johnson, the elusive one. Yolanda, along with Pam, Indigo and myself were all the names left in the box by the time we'd finished. Soon, all of our asses would be blowing in the wind with plenty of hidden secrets to go around!

# Naked 9

The trip home in the wee hours of the morning was as much annoying for Eddie as it was mystifying for Ray, who couldn't be sure if the man he'd met at *The Blue Bird* was an angelic spirit sent to save him or just a drunken figment of his imagination. Either way, it was hopeless for Eddie to figure out and Ray to explain. Therefore, neither said anything. Not a word. By the time they got home, the house was already full of anxiety and unspoken tension. He and Ray's obvious frustration easily fit the mood of the morning.

"Hey, what's going on in here," Eddie asked, his baritone voice laced with a bit of annoyance as the two walked through the door.

The conversation caused Charlotte to wake. And, soon thereafter, Shalamar raised her head from the tightly balled blanket she'd used as a pillow. First she saw Charlotte, who was getting up and moving towards the kitchen. Then, she quickly followed suit. Before I knew it, everyone else came.

After the four gathered and confronted us, I felt a nerve twitch in my forehead; I knew there would be trouble. Everybody had a look on their faces like I somehow had all the answers. Malik was now slouched over the countertop, a signature away from an asylum. I knew he didn't want to talk anymore about the dark side of his life. The rest of that conversation would take place, if ever, at another point in time.

The three women standing over us were curious as dicks in a whorehouse. Their questions fast and furious, each demanding to be answered before I could think of an appropriate lie to explain the morning's events. Finally, in an effort to keep my sanity, I offered what I deemed was the only right thing to do to calm everyone; I explained again what the box of folders was and how we'd found ourselves in this position.

The explanation scared the hell out of them. I guess the thought of something like this actually happening in real life was just too extraordinary, and better kept to the movies or squeezed between the pages of a good novel. But to happen here, to us. Well, it just couldn't be happening! Now the question became, what were we prepared to do to keep this from destroying us?

First though, they wanted to know the names on the remaining folders inside the box and what was inside them. Everyone has a hidden chest full of secrets, hurt, pain, indiscretions, regrets and stupidity leading to bad decisions, which makes us human. None of those I would personally want to come in the middle of my life and haunt me again, after I'd comfortably put them away in a locked part of my soul. It was the same for the others, who already chose to have selective memories forgetting what they didn't want to remember, or forgiving themselves for ones they did.

# N a k e d 10

T.J. thought carefully about the night he'd spent with the delightfully charismatic woman he'd met years earlier at a small showing of his artwork. It was at a local gallery on the North Side. He didn't know why his mind had revisited that moment. Maybe, the crazy danger we now found ourselves in at Eddie's gave him a hard-on or something. Whatever it was, the woman had left quite an impression on T.J., who always fancied her for as long as we'd been friends, which was going on ten years.

To her credit, she loved him with an equal amount of hard felt passion. "There's just something irresistible about a man of the arts," I remembered her telling me after I'd inquired one day why she was so obsessed with him.

The woman's image was firmly stuck inside his cranium, identified only by T.J.'s vivid imagination of all the naughty details of their evenings together. A particular one came to mind.

Her legs were long, and easily wrapped around his waist when she straddled him. They laid on the side of a hill just below the surface of the street. He held her firmly by the waist at first. Then after a slow, wet kiss, his hands moved down her side, led by his long fingers gently rubbing the moist entrance of her life giver. He inserted one of them and she immediately responded to him with her legs opened. His finger reached deeper inside her. With each moment and gentle thrust, the quicker her fluids wetted his touch. He rubbed his hands on her curvy hips and used his thumbs to raise the pale blue dress she wore.

She took out his manhood, which was now solid with lust and eagerly waiting to intrude on her soft kitten. She lifted her hips and held him as she guided his manhood inside of her. Her dress was now pulled above her waist, exposing the smooth cocoa ass that rested on his lap. Her knees positioned outside of his, slow circular grinds were a testament to the ecstasy they both felt.

The night was uncommonly warm for the season. It was autumn on the cool grass of the park, but the warm breeze said spring and the passion felt like summer. Their embrace was a perfect fit. Both had the same thin frame. Therefore, when they intertwined, it was like their bodies were made for each other.

When he came the first time, it forced his body into an uncontrollable throb. He clinched the ground to brace himself to lift his own hips to meet hers. T.J. and the woman sizzled! Riding each other wildly as if their bodies were linked together becoming one. Their movements became so intense he lifted his hips high off of the ground and her folded legs dangled freely on each side of him. His movements took complete control of her.

She firmly placed her hands around his waist to brace herself. Then, she arched her back and began to pump back and forth. Her head freely fell back and each of the strokes with her hips became quicker and more intense than the other. T.J. held his position steady and she continued until they both grunted an exhilarating scream that allowed their bodies to release the pleasure each held inside them. They collapsed from the rhythm and laid together holding each other tightly, with his still firm penis resting inside of her. Their eyes closed, and the warm breeze passed against their faces once again.

* * *

T.J.'s story was compelling. In fact, at the time he told it, I was ready to find Ms. "Unknown" and create my own memories. However, that was five years ago. Now those thoughts of pleasantries were only a way to escape the moment.

Maybe, it was T.J.'s *crackhead* mother, who frequently turned tricks to buy dime rocks when he was a child that caused him to have a taste for exotic pleasures more than the rest of us. Or even his player father, who managed to keep a flock of young women half his age on standby and eager to share the sheets with him. They hung on every word of his smooth tongue and stuck to his offbeat personality like glue. Whichever it was, there would be many more sweet lustful memories sweeping through T.J.'s mind, but he came into the kitchen without sharing any. His attention instead was on what was going on with us, after listening to the loud outbursts in Eddie's since five in the morning.

"May I ask, what the hell is going on in here," T.J. asked. "Eddie, what is all of this shit about?"

"All I know it's something to do with the box sitting over there and those folders. The rest you need to ask him," pointing in my direction.

"Look," I responded. "You already know just about all there is to know. We're being blackmailed."

"Blackmailed! With what?" asked T.J.

"These," I answered, pointing to the box with my folder still resting on the floor next to me. He saw it. Then I remembered the reason I set it there in the first place was to avoid anyone seeing it, at least not just yet. My little oversight would have to be smoothed over with some real smooth talk.

"That folder would be..." questioned T.J., who I thought was on to me.

"It would be what all of these are," I said. "Ghosts! Ghosts, that should have stayed hidden and buried in the past. Instead, we're getting blackmailed by them."

"By the looks on your faces, I must have missed something," he said.

"No," interrupted Malik. "You didn't miss a damn thing!" A large frown came about his face.

"Well, fucking excuse me," replied T.J. "Must have been serious. At any rate, I don't much believe in ghosts. I tend to subscribe to the notion I live my life to the fullest of each day's possibilities. Therefore, each day becomes what it becomes. It frees me from regrets and ghosts that could come back to bite me in the ass when I least expect them. I know it may sound a bit calculated considering the many uncertainties of life. Shit, who can control them? I just let life flow."

"What are you saying," Ray asked. "You ain't got nothing in your past you want to forget? Or even regret?"

"That's a different type of thing," T.J. said, concerned about what if a folder would divulge his life. "Do I have any regrets? The answer is no. Are there parts of my life that have been bruised? Yes, there are. Can I change them? No."

"Please!" shouted Ray. "You're just full of a bunch of smooth talk. You walk around like you don't give a bird's shit about any damn thing. I bet you got a closet full of skeletons you hide."

"We don't need to go there or anywhere close to there," I said stepping in. "Ray, this ain't about T.J. And T.J., I think you're a very lucky man if you can have that kind of reverence and nonchalant love of life. Both of you brothers need to quit it and focus on what's really going on."

"All right," said T.J. "All right. I'll shut up. I'm not trying to start no trouble. Looks like there's already plenty of that."

"Yeah, it is," I said. "Whether your know it or not, you're part of it too." Even though he didn't have his name on a folder, he was still very much involved.

"What?" he asked boldly. "My name's on one of those things?"

"No, it's not," I said. "Not yet anyway."

"Are you sure? Never mind. It doesn't matter. I don't have nothing to be ashamed of. Furthermore, I don't have nothing to do with this shit."

"Oh yes you do," I corrected. "These people don't give a rat's ass about that. All they know is, you know us. As far as they're concerned, you could be just as involved as we are. Morgan and Detective Hall are only concerned with getting the video and diary back in their possession. Who they choose to implicate in a blackmail conspiracy is probably irrelevant. If that changes, and more people need to be dealt with to get what they want, then so be it."

I preached, like I really knew how the criminal mind worked. Maybe I did? It was all common sense to me. A freaky, high-rolling Senator caught on tape and an ass kissing son-of-a-bitch pulling all the strings. They each would stop at nothing to finish this.

I knew T.J. pretty much didn't care what was going on except out of curiosity. He had been friends with most of us for several years. I think he and Eric went back the furthest, twelve years. I met him a year or two after that. He was a young skinny punk with a lot of personality and a big mouth.

Eric met T.J. at an art gallery in Atlanta when he was there for a sales convention. Since then, they had become beer and wine buddies, who enjoyed chasing women and listening to café jazz together in local lounges, despite their six year age difference. The differential was valuable to their continued friendship. T.J.'s self-centered immaturity needed the conscious guidance of a friend like Eric. In return, he provided Eric with the colorful life of an artist, although he still had issues with T.J.'s habitual weed smoking and frequent estranged relationships.

Therefore, Eric ignored the invitation to smoke and dismissed T.J.'s several attempts at encouraging him to rekindle his seven-year relationship with his ex-girlfriend, Linda. She was well aware of T.J.'s bad influences. Not to mention, she was an aspiring artist herself and resented with every fiber of her being, T.J.'s talent and passion.

\* \* \*

It was now official. We had no way out. Forty-eight hours had passed, and we still had no idea of what we were going to do, how we were going to do it, or if we could do anything at all. That's right, nobody knew a damn thing! Time was not on our side. Emotions were falling all over the place. Malik was still very much angry; Nicole saddened by her recounts; and Indigo disappointed at us being forced to cancel the wedding.

The drama with the folders had taken its toll, yet we had more to go. Eddie crossed the line and insisted he be allowed to read the next one. It was a demand I couldn't believe he'd made. After all, it wasn't his soul packaged neatly to devastate his very existence as a man. Did he care? I'm sure he did. It didn't matter if he was gay or not. Coming out openly with his sexual orientation might have been humiliating in some way, but couldn't possibly compare to the rest of his life that he didn't, wouldn't, and couldn't dare share with the rest of the world.

Charlotte, Shalamar, and Indigo stared at me. I was obviously still shaken from the night before at nearly having my ass shot down. It was the closest I had ever been to having my life taken from me. Indigo's prayers had protected me-at least this time. Our faith hadn't slipped, but the forces of evil were working overtime to defeat us. Last night proved that. But despite the devil's fresh flame burning for me, this was going to be finished one way or another with us winning. Pam was going to be found somehow, some way. It was only a matter of time.

Time. There was that word again. The only asset we didn't have very much of.

We gathered in the kitchen, which had begun to be headquarters for us. We tried to figure out what we needed to do to gain control of this madness. First, we concluded immediately no matter what, we absolutely had to find that bitch, Pam! Then almost as quickly as we came up with that no-brainer, when the question of how was raised, I heard and felt the air rush right out of the room again.

"I don't know either," replied Eddie. He continued to anticipate the next folder being read.

"Well, where was she last seen?"

"Yeah, what happened after the shooting?" Everyone seemed to want more information.

"All I know," I said, "is she was taken to the same hospital as Kayra, who was dead on arrival. I knew that for a fact. When I got there she was already pronounced. I didn't wait around for anything about Pam or anybody else. Later, I just assumed Pam didn't make it through, either. It was probably wishful thinking. Maybe I was wrong and she wasn't taken there. I assumed she was. Maybe that might be the first place to start looking."

"Okay," said Indigo. "Here's what we're going to do. Karen, get on the phone and contact the hospital. What was the name?"

"I believe that it was Lord of Peace Memorial," I said. "The one on the south side off of the lake."

"Karen, see how far back their records go," Indigo said. "I know they keep track of everybody who still owes their butts money. If we're lucky, hopefully Pam left behind an unpaid bill. Insurance companies only cover so much; the rest is the patient's obligation. If our dear Pam stays true to character, they're as anxious to find her as we are!"

"All right," I said. "All right! Let's go then." I was being pressed by the others to start our investigation by going to the hospital where Pam had been admitted three years earlier. It might have been a long shot, but it was the only one we had. Everything else had turned to shit.

"So, what's up," asked Eric. "What are we going to do?"

"Didn't you hear? We're getting the hell out of here," said Shalamar, speaking up for the first time. Her patience had grown thin and whether she knew it or not, she slowly became one of us.

"Look," I said. "I think the best thing to do is to wait here."

"Wait for what," Indigo differed. "Wait for the next delivery?"

"Shit," Eric said frustrated. "The next time it might be more than a damn folder. I don't care what's in them. It can and will get a lot worse. Believe me."

"Easy for you to say," Malik said. "Let's see your fuckin' name on one of them things, and we'll see how worse it can get. All you've got to do is sit your ass on that counter and watch. It's the rest of us who got to deal with this shit."

"Stop it, Malik," said Indigo. "We need to go. Are you coming or what? When we leave the hospital, I think it would be a good idea if we stopped by Jasmine's to see if someone there knows something."

I was surprised as hell at Indigo's suggestion. Over the past couple of years, she had resisted the notion to ever go to that place. With that in mind, I insisted Shalamar and Indigo go to the hospital. Cedric, Tarnisha and Karen stayed at Eddie's I sent Eddie to the police station to see what he could find. Nicole, Charlotte, Eric and Malik came with me to Jasmine's. The only person who might've still been there was Special K., the comic I remembered from before.

\* \* \*

It had been almost four days since our ordeal first started with the first call from Detective Hall. We were all in this together. Those who had plans to return home would just have to make other arrangements.

# Naked 11

"Shh," said Charlotte. "Listen." Her request did nothing to help our already fragile nerves.

"What?" I asked wondering what the hell she was talking about now.

"Hear it?" she continued, "Y'all don't know about good music. Listen to that. Phat Cat Players is the shit! Ever hear their song, *Sundress*? Listen to the words."

"How in the..."

"That's what I'm talking about," she bellowed after hearing some of the lyrics. "You go boy! *'I'll be that sundress in the breeze from the north.'* Ooh, let me stop."

"You act like you're getting a hard-on," laughed Eric. "Been a while since you've been in a club?"

Eric was a fool if I heard or saw one. He hadn't offered anything worthwhile or positive to our immediate situation and after his remark, it wasn't in any danger of being changing.

"Fool, I just enjoy good, solid music." Charlotte replied.

Cedric began singing the theme music to the show "Solid Gold". That got us all going.

"Good one," Charlotte said. "You're hating 'cause you can't relate. He's singing about some real shit."

"Charlotte, you wouldn't know real shit if you stepped in it," joked Eric.

"Anyway," she countered. "Ya'll got to get this CD. It reflects what making music is all about to me. Fuck you very much, Eric."

"I wonder if the same comedian still works this joint? What was his name?" asked Nicole.

"Special K., I believe it was," answered Malik. "What are we doing here, Jake?"

I wanted to answer. But to tell you the truth, I didn't really know either. It seemed like only yesterday Malik and I had been in that club. We were both surprised it was still open. Black folks can't seem to have a steady place to party for more than a year or two before it's shut down. Not true for Jasmine's. It was there and still beautiful as ever. The colors changed a bit, but it still reflected elegance.

"I think you're right," I said. "Matter of fact, is that him over there by the table next to the stage?"

"Yeah," said Malik. "Go say 'what's up'?"

"You think I should?"

"You want information, don't you? You're going to have to do something."

"That's for damn sure," I said. And with that, I made my move.

* * *

"What's up, my brother?" Special K. greeted me as I approached him. "I remember you," he continued. "You're the brother, who got caught up at the bar a couple of years ago. That shit don't happen too much in here, that's probably why I remember you." He repeated. What's your name, bro'?"

"Jake," I said. "Jake Alexander."

"Jake," he repeated. "Okay. Of course. I'm Special K. Nice meeting you."

"Same here," I said, not knowing if I was glad he remembered me or not.

"I know you might like my show and all, but you look like you've got something else on your mind. Just kidding! What can the K. do for you, brother Jake?

"We need some information," I told him.

"Information about what? Who is this *we*?"

"The *we* are my friends and I. The information we need is about someone we knew."

"Look, man," Special K. said. "I know what you're looking to hear, but I grew up on the South Side. I didn't survive all of those years by sharing information with folks. Especially, folks I didn't know."

"I understand, man," I said, trying to ease his fears.

"But, look. This is about a girl named Pam. Pam Johnson. She was one of the chicks that were here when all of that stuff happened with me. She was the short chick with the big mouth. Come on. You've got to remember her?"

"Funny color hair," he asked. "Kinda' cute?"

"Yeah," I said. "The hair for sure. Cute? Well…"

"Man," he said, "if it's the girl I'm thinking about, she was fine! All them chicks were pretty straight. You roll pretty well there, boy."

"Okay," I said. "Okay, that's the one. Have you seen her again?"

"Naw. If I'd seen her you would know. I'd have her fine butt right here."

"You think somebody else might know her or have seen her around?

"Naw, man. I told you I ain't seen her, and I don't know nobody that's down with her. Why? What's going on? Why you looking for this chick?"

"Somebody we knew was murdered, and we think Pam might have something to do with it, or at least know something. We just want to find her and ask some questions."

"What? You Five-O?"

"Police? Hell no! I'm a friend trying to help. I just need some answers. That's all."

"Wish I could help. But, stay for my show and maybe we can talk later."

"Are you sure you don't know anybody that could help? Somebody? Anybody? Anything?"

"I told you. Stay for the show. I'll think about it and we'll talk later."

"I'll stick around for a little while. I hope you can give us something worth waiting for."

"I'll check with you later, man. Peace."

After our brief conversation, Special K. turned and headed backstage to prepare for his performance later that evening. I began to feel just a small sense of hopefulness, although it was slim. Very slim. I wasn't sure if K. knew something or not, it seemed like at least he was willing to do what he could. I relayed what I'd found out to the others. They were as disappointed as I was that we didn't get more concrete and useful information. But just as I did, they became optimistic maybe, somehow, things would change later and we'd find out more. We all agreed to stay and see what happened.

Moments later Special K. took the stage. When I saw him enter it was déjà vu. The last time Malik and I came here it was the beginning of the end of life, as we knew it. I could picture Pam and Kayra sitting here. And right over there, as if it were just yesterday, I stood at the bar looking at a face that I still couldn't get out of my mind: Yolanda's. She was Nicole's old friend and was with her the night Malika and I met them here. Thoughts of her danced around in my head. Her enticing flirtation still stimulated me, despite Kayra's beautiful soft voice ringing clearly in my ears. I could hear her whispers as her head rested on my shoulders. I felt the smooth skin of her cheeks pressing up against mine. Why would I cheat on her with Yolanda was a bad mistake and I take full responsibilty for it. But she was cool and I learned a lot from the time we spent together.

My heart cried at the realization Kayra was gone. Killed senselessly because of Pam. Oh, I knew I was partly to blame. After all, had I not acted like a damn fool, and had a case of temporary insanity when I got caught up with Yolanda, maybe none of this would've happened. I've tried not being too hard on myself because there was a lot of other shit going on in her life that contributed to her death. But, somehow, I couldn't help but feel Kayra might have still been alive if it weren't for me.

Regardless of how dramatic I was feeling, one thing remained certain; Jasmine's still rocked! The music felt good. I looked, and I didn't see one person standing still. It was something hypnotic about the place. It oozed sexiness.

Malik and Charlotte became invisible and lost themselves in the midst of the crowd. Nicole had given

Charlotte permission to steal him to escort her to the bar. Nicole stayed next to me, and we talked. She told me how things had been between her and Malik. The secret she'd kept hidden had been a problem, she admitted. They were married for only two short years, and it had been rough. A claim she confessed reluctantly.

They loved each other very much and were living a good life together. He had worked his way up into a management position after going back to school to earn a degree in Accounting. Now he headed a regional accounting department for a national computer software manufacturer. Nicole was the district Human Resources supervisor for the company. There were no kids to distract them or to occupy their time. As I saw it, they had every opportunity to get whatever was ailing their relationship right. They seemed like they wanted to.

Nicole's biggest vice was she became emotional over the smallest of things. Her once free-flowing conversations now consisted of mumbles. And many times, she found herself wishing she could be alone. Unfortunately for their relationship, this happened in the bedroom too, where Malik's warm embraces felt like cold handshakes and his kisses unwanted nuisances. Malik recently began discussing starting a family and having their first child together. At thirty-three years old, he thought it was time to overcome the fear of fatherhood after the way his father mistreated and violated him. For years Malik he caged those things in his life. The folders just opened a door that was already cracked.

Nicole made herself forget her rape, and together these two tortured souls attempted their best at making their marriage work. Malik made some progress in controlling his hot temper, which was primarily due to extended periods of unemployment and little money. All wasn't bad, though. They frequently laughed together, especially after Malik lost his excessive preoccupation with leading a Black resistance movement all by himself. It was a drive which added a jolt to his life. A bright spot of passion he use to drive a stronger self-esteem as a man.

\* \* \*

The house lights dimmed and the colorful stage lights became the focus of everyone's attention. The anticipation mounted waiting for the night's main attraction. Special K. had become quite a star over the past three years; receiving national acclaim after a stellar performance at a comic festival in the Bahamas. Black Entertainment Television sponsored the event. Soon after, Movie Box Network came calling and offered a One-Night-Stand special performance. Despite all the new found opportunties, it was the love Special K. received at Jasmine's that he loved the most. K. started there when the club opened four years ago. It had been a special training ground for him, where he learned and perfected the craft of comedy. He knew however, he would one day be a bird thrown from the nest left to soar the greater skies. The upcoming week was scheduled to be his last performance at Jasmine's. The offers were pouring in, and he figured it was time to get the gettin' while the gettin' was good. If I'm not mistaken, he was going to move to Los Angeles the following month, an expense included in one of the deals he'd contracted, of course. His manager was also a long time girlfriend who he'd met growing up in Chicago. She was now his wife and did a more than adequate job of managing his business affairs. How they balanced the grueling aspects of his career with the demands of a relationship was a mystery. It worked even though at thirty-seven, K. was still in his sexual prime. He loved flirting with women at his shows and made it a part of his act. Although no matter what, he was going home to his wife, Cynthia. Straight home. No midnight creeps and no weekend disappearing acts. His commitment was wise considering she controlled his money. I tipped my hat to the wisdom.

Somehow, I knew that night's performance would be very special. I was glad to see him blow up and in some strange way, I felt a part of his success. I was hopeful before the night was over with, he would be a part of helping us find Pam, the real reason we were really there in the first place. It was hard remembering that fact in all of the heightened anticipation for the act. When K. came on stage the crowd roared. The ovation lasted several minutes and he soaked up every moment. Clean and the sharp. He changed into a suit only five minutes before show time. The time was well spent. The rest of the audience agreed when they saw him.

"What's up, everybody," he began. "Here we go again. Another night with y'all asses. Damn! Ain't that some shit! Next week, will be it b-baabbyy! Before I go though, I really gotta' thank y'all for the love and support y'all have always given me here at Jasmine's. Go 'head and give yo' selves a round of applause. Soak it all up. 'Cause you know it's the last time yo' ass gone ever and...I do mean *ever* gon' get recognized!"

The packed house responded with thunderous applause and laughter. The smiles were generous and K. appreciated the recognition of their support. Chicago always had a reputation for not fully supporting its own talent. Whether fact or fiction, tonight it didn't matter.

After another five minutes passed, he started in on some guy in the audience he'd seen was drunk and had accidentally knocked over a tray carried by one of the beautiful waitresses.

"Now would you looka' here? Look at this drunk ass muthafucka here," he began. "I guess "Woodrow" forgot, *when to say when*. Knocking drinks over and shit. Probably can't afford a can of coke."

"Me?" the drunk guy flapped.

"Yeah, you. Yo' drunk ass got money to pay for those drinks? Or do we need to turn yo' ass upside down to shake out what's left of yo' paycheck? You do work?

"Yeah, I work!" He yells back.

"What job you got? Denny's? Your ass don't have no money. They email your check! Crown Royal bag carrying ass."

"Here's my Crown Royal bag, right here," the guy said, pointing to his crotch.

"Dude, that ain't no Crown Royal bag, it's a fuckin' cry for help!"

The crowd was in stitches.

"Is that your man, little lady?" K. asked the woman sitting at the table with the drunk.

"Yes."

"Poor baby," he said shaking his head. "I guess there is somebody for everybody."

"I love you!" a woman shouted from the back of the room.

"Girl, now you know I'm a married man," he said back. "Put your drawz back on, girl. My wife told me if I brought back any more panties from a show...they'd better be from Victoria's Secret. And those look like Victoria done told!"

Another voice yelled, "Take it off, K." Then a chant of "Take it off! Take it off!" began.

K. only got as far as his jacket off. He had made it to the big time. Losing over fifty pounds to boast the six-pack he sported and which could be seen through his fitted shirt. He had an image to project now that he was going national. All the screaming ladies noticed the new physique and wanted to see it. K. definitely wanted to show it. I was caught up in all the excitement, too, but I wished he'd hurry up so we could get to the real business and purpose of our visit. Despite my eagerness to get what I came for, I found it hard to be mad at him. It was his night and our business wasn't his, at least that's what I came in thinking.

Charlotte and Malik made their way back to where we were standing before. Nicole and I met up, and we all gathered around the end of the bar located in the front corner, just to the right of the stage. We didn't sit, but stood anxious in the shadows of the dimmed lights waiting for K. to finish doing his thing. He signaled to the stage manager with a nod, which meant he was ready to begin.

"Now you know I've got to start on black folks," he said. "I was gonna' pick on *White America*. Nah. That's too easy. It's y'all in here that really need to get y'all shit together. If I hear one more syllable in front of "Eesha or "Meeka, Lord knows I'm gonna' scream! Doneesha! Shemeeka! Did black flok run out of names or what? I'm gonna' get rich and start a new lottery, just like the regular lottery you go down to the cotner and buy a ticket for. But this one will be a scratch off ticket of those weird black folk names. Better yet, how about a drawing every week on channel nine? The next time Lil' Boo gets locked up or Ree Ree has a baby, you can go down to the liquor store and put two dollars on Shawnvetta, or Condeisha and wait for the drawing to see what name comes up that week."

The audience went ballistic with laughter. Everybody's rolling over in their chair. I turned to Malik.

"What you say," I asked.

"I said he still got it," he shouted.

"He sure does," I agreed. "I wonder what he has? Or should I say, knows?"

"No kidding."

Despite the subject matter of our conversation, we still managed to enjoy the night. It felt good to laugh, and it kept us from crying.

The enthusiasm he received during the night was more satisfying than any performance he'd had done before. Maybe, with the exception of his first one. Since this was nearing the end of his era at Jasmine's, his closing moments would be more than memorable. As he prepared to leave the stage, our anticipation grew feverishly.

"Is it me, or because I'm just a man," he asked the audience. "But guys ain't too clean when it comes to doing chores at home. We'll be rushing, trying to look at the game and shit. I do pretty good around the house for a guy. I mean, at least I clean. 'Cause you know a man will stick his finger up his ass, scratch his prostate, then go in the cabinets getting plates and glasses then sit his ass back down and look at the game. Or worse, go to the refrigerator like ain't shit happened. He'll pick up another fork out the damn dishwater. Thanks everybody. Y'all are wonderful! I love you! Thank you, Jasmine's."

We used the distraction of the applauding to make our way backstage. Before we got there, we were stopped by a tall, burly brother wearing a way too tight suit and schoolboy glasses. He was in charge of security and inquired why we were trying to get somewhere we didn't belong. I tried explaining K. agreed to talk. I didn't say about what, only we were fans of his and had spoken to him earlier before the show. He didn't seem to care much for my explanation. I guess the five of us looked like a bunch of groupies or something to him. Eric and I didn't crack a smile and maybe even looked a bit confrontational. Hell, we had serious issues to resolve and no time for more foolishness. Charlotte, Nicole and Malik might've been pleasant enough under normal circumstances to help our cause, but that night wasn't the time. "Mr. Burly" insisted we remove ourselves from the premises or he would have to do it for us. Before things got ugly, we heard a rich baritone voice from behind the guard.

"It's okay, Butter," K. said. "They're with me."

"Butter?" Malik looked at me and we shrugged our shoulders simultaneously.

"What a name," I thought. Especially for somebody who acted tough and looked more like a Bruce. How he got such a nickname was beyond me. I guessed that would be a question for another place and time. Either way, with that pushed to the side, we were glad to hear K.'s voice. The man still acted like he didn't want to let us by. Without saying another word, he stared and grunted when we passed him on our way to the backstage entrance.

"Butter," called K. "I told you it's all right. Come on, y'all."

"See ya...Butter," said Malik sarcastically.

We enjoyed the taunt as we walked by. I smirked but dared not laugh at the comment. I had wanted to say something, myself. I thought better of the idea because I didn't want to make matters worse and maybe even ruin our chance to get whatever information K. might give us. But I was glad as hell Malik had the balls to say what I didn't.

"Sorry 'bout that," K. apologized. "There's been a lot of crazy folks around here lately, and Butter can sometimes get a little overzealous. But, he's a damn good bodyguard and does his job well."

"Okay," I said. "Forget it." Giving in to the temptation, I just had to ask. "What's with the name?"

"Who," K. asked. "Butter?" He felicitated surprise then burst out laughing. "I figured you'd ask. Everybody kinda' trips about that."

"So," I relegated.

"Spit it out, and let's get on with this," said Charlotte

frustrated and impatient.

We all looked back at her with eyebrows raised to signify a collective, 'you go, girl!'

"His name is Butterfield. We grew up together in the projects on the South Side. His mother died when he was eight. After that, he came to live with us. I don't know why his mother named him that. Now, come with me."

\* \* \*

The hallway was cold and pungent. It was dim with only a single ceiling fan for light. He led us nearly fifty feet from where we were inside the club. There were several doors including three private *champagne rooms*. I couldn't resist peeking inside one to see if there really was sex in the *champagne room*. Charlotte and Eric were curious, too.

They followed me as I stopped at one of the tinted doors. There was a gold-plated sign in the center. I could see the color reflecting from the dim light. I leaned closer and read, '*For Ballers Only*'. K. kept walking in front of us and didn't notice the quick detour we'd made. Nicole held Malik in check and stopped him from coming with us. I cracked the door open and heard soft music playing.

"I can't see, man." Eric complained hastily because he couldn't get his head in far enough to get his peek on.

"Me, neither," said Charlotte. She's pissed.

"Shhh," I whispered.

We pushed the door open about three-quarters of the way, sticking our heads inside the door as far as we could.

"Woo," whispered Eric.

"Damn!" Charlotte couldn't hold back her satisfaction.

"Mmmm," I mumbled before any words could come out of my mouth.

"Guess there is sex in the *Champagne Room*," laughed Eric.

We quickly closed the door without disturbing the occupants inside and raced to catch up to the others who hadn't even noticed we were missing.

"Here we are," said K. "Follow me."

We came to the gold-plated door with his name clearly marked, *Special K.* Charlotte couldn't control her staring as we walked inside the elegant dressing room.

"Must be nice being a rising star," she said. "You single? No, that's right. You've got a woman. Just kidding."

"Is that really important," asked K. "This shit ain't about nothing. Life can be a scary thing. Facing it and being strong in the journey. Especially, trying not to let yourself think about negative things happening like, getting older, death, even life itself. Damn near can go crazy just existing when you face the reality of it all. A rising star? Hum, what does that really mean? Almost nothing."

I thought for a moment, pondering the meaning of the

enlightening words spoken with an eerie honesty. The truth struck home. It scared the hell out of me before I began thinking more positively.

"Means you're blessed," I said in response to his observation.

"I'd like to have a blessing or two," replied Eric.

"So would I," chimed Charlotte.

"Have a seat," K. demanded. "All of you. Just sit the hell down."

"Guess we'll be sitting now," smarted Eric.

Charlotte reached for a purple chair near the large mirror and immediately sat. Eric flopped on the thick cushioned couch. Nicole and I remained standing, leaning against the back wall. K. walked to where he was most comfortable. He swirled the blue captain chair, around and eased himself onto the contours he'd made from the countless times he'd sat there before. He spoke quietly at first. His words bounced around with nervousness, but we still clung to each one as if it would be the last.

"I told you all you need to know," he began. "Hall is down with the big boys. The Senator is his boss and the chief of Chicago's Finest is his biggest crook. The chief and Hall use to work together when they were both with the Feds in DC. From what I hear, they got next to the world's most powerful men. They scratched a lot of backs and got a lot of favors pulled in return."

"Then some shit jumped off and they both found themselves reassigned to city positions with their reputations ruined. What he's doing here in Chicago? I don't know, man. Either he followed the chief or he's still connected from his DC days. Whatever the case, he's on Senator Morgan's security staff. The Senator is an Illinois boy from the South Side of Chicago. That's it. As far as the Pam chick, I don't know what her story is. I heard she was a wild one, and ain't no telling what she was into. I haven't seen her since you were here three years ago."

"Wait a minute," demanded Malik. "How do you know so damn much? You are supposed to be telling jokes and shit."

"Thank you." said Charlotte. "I'm sitting here thinking 'what?'"

"I'm hip," I said. "I thought it was just me thinking that. K.? You down with them or what?"

"Hey, I was trying to stay out of this, but you all kept insisting. I only know about this Hall dude because he needed extra security last year when the Senator came to Chicago. And..."

"And, don't tell us," Malik interrupted wryly. "Butter there was one of the chosen ones?"

"Yeah, he got the job. Trust me; he's been doing this a long time and knows a few people himself. I guess Butter used what he knew to find out what he knows."

"Butter," said Nicole. "Where is he?"

"Nope," K. said shaking his head. "He works for me, and he ain't got nothing to say. I'm not going to involve him in your mess. What he told me was in strict confidence. I shouldn't be telling you none of this. All I got to say is find that chick you're looking for and give those folks what they want. Leave me and my people out of it."

"Bullshit," Eric shouted. "This is all bullshit!"

"Whatever, man," replied K.

"How does this help us," asked Nicole. "We still don't know where she is."

"It doesn't," said Eric.

Before anyone answered, the door opened. It swung quick and with purpose. It was Butter.

"Time to go, K.," he said. "Let's get out of here. Now."

"I gotta' go. I've told you what I know."

"Wait," I said not knowing why.

"That's it, man. I'm gone."

# Naked 12

Around one thirty that afternoon the phone rang, just as Jana was preparing for lunch. She quickly picked up the receiver. "Hello."

"Jana?"

"Yeah."

"It's me."

"Hey! Shhh. Wait a minute until I go to the back," whispered Jana.

She leaned over and explained to her anxious client her absence would be brief. Before Jana left to go to the back she wrapped a large white towel around the woman's neck. It was warm and felt good as it was lifted over her hair to dry it.

"There," she said. "That should hold you. Girls, I got to go take this call. I'll be right back."

Jana grabbed the phone again and walked to the back as

quickly as she could. The salon's lounge was spacious and private with the one door to the entrance heavy and solid. The inside contained two sofas, a huge round coffee table and an oak desk where she sat and began her private conversation with the young woman on the other end.

"How are you? Any progress?"

"I can't do this," the woman responded. "I just can't do this!"

"Calm down!" Jana demanded. "What's wrong? Tell me what happened?"

"They're going to kill us! Do you hear me? They're going to kill us!"

"Who?" asked Jana. "I told you, nobody's going to hurt you. Tell me who you're talking about. Damn it! Get your shit together and tell me what the hell is going on!" Jana looked around after realizing how loud she'd become.

"It's them!"

"Them, who?" Jana still was in the dark.

"The Detective and his crew!"

* * *

Two suited men descended the flight of stairs leading from the station doors. Their strides were swift while they maintained their stone-faced looks and kept their eyes forward. When they approached Eddie near his vandalized truck, they didn't even look in his direction. T he taller of the two men did use his extremely broad shoulders to brush up against Eddie, bumping him enough to make him stumble against his truck. Prior to the rude contact, Eddie wanted to ask for help. But, after he looked at the men's faces, he knew immediately it wouldn't be such a good idea. When they damn near knocked his ass down as they marched by, it was confirmed. When the shorter of the two men turned and gave him a long hard stare, it was obvious their intention was to send a message.

Before Eddie could heed to it and get the hell out of there, he turned to face Detective Hall standing in his way. His arm stretched and a large hand spread across the door of Eddie's truck holding it in place.

"Look, you punk," said the Detective. "Get your sweet little ass out of here and don't bring it back. Come here again, and I'll shoot you where you stand. Tell your friend he's running out of time. The other day was just a warning. Next time, we won't miss. I'll personally make sure of it. I got a personal score to settle with him, anyway." Afterwards, Hall gently pinched his nose adjusting it into place.

Eddie didn't speak a word. Detective Hall lifted his large hand from the door, turned, and walked away. Eddie opened it, jumped in, and started his truck as fast as he could. The tires screeched and the remaining loose glass fell from the windshield as he sped off. Eddie looked like a man who'd just robbed a bank and was in a high-speed chase from the law.

\* \* \*

The highway was almost deserted. It was late, and Eddie's *bat-out-of-hell* escape went almost unnoticed by the few other motorists on the road. He got to the next highway exit and immediately pulled over at a gas station, after checking his rearview mirror again to see if he was safe. For the time being, he was. No one had followed him. The night was brisk, and the crisp air stung whenever the breeze grazed his open wounds.

"Damn! Those crazy sons-of-bitches are trying to kill me! I got to get my ass out of here." Eddie was exhausted and exasperated. The once cool, gentle night breeze became a cold roaring wind making driving almost impossible with a missing windshield-especially at highway speed. Even at the forty-five miles an hour minimum, the *Chicago Hawk* infiltrated the interior with the strength of a small tornado, forcing Eddie to fight to keep his head up long enough to see the road. Finally, he gave up and pulled over again. Two headlights flashed behind him. Three men jumped out and bumrushed Eddie's truck from the front. One of the men was humongous. The others...just huge.

They yanked Eddie out of the truck, taped his mouth with duct tape, and threw a heavy black hood over his head. A thin rope held the hood in place around Eddie's throat. It was snuggled tightly against his Adam's apple. The pressure almost choked him. He gasped for air, and each breath seemed to get shorter than the one before. It was like trying to breathe through a bent straw. Eddie struggled as best he could, but the team of men controlled his every move. One man held his ankles while another grabbed him about the neck. They took him to the waiting van, opened a rear door, and tossed him inside. The door barreled close with the men hopping in front, then they drove off disappearing into the darkness of the night.

# N a k e d    13

Senator Morgan sat restless at his desk. He was in Washington, and time was beginning to run out. It had been almost two weeks since he'd given Detective Hall the assignment of finding Pam Johnson and recovering the evidence that would be sure to destroy his run for the Presidency of the United States. He was a black man. His extremely light complexion might possibly have helped play that fact down somewhat, but in a political campaign it was certainly not enough to overcome any scandals. The Republican Party leaders would have a field day,  as well as his own Democratic colleagues, not to mention his supporters back home. If he stood any chance at all, it had to be on the strength of an almost blemish-free campaign record. The new Senate leader, who was responsible for Morgan's only negative record in his twelve years in office was from a noted bigot from Iowa. One insider reported overhearing a comment made by him, which essentially demonized a fellow Senator from California as a nigger lover and the Senate leader made no bones he would do everything in his political power to make him pay for his sensitivities towards minorities and his friendships with them.

Morgan grew up on the outside of Chicago. But, it wasn't until he moved for a brief four years to Memphis he discovered an eagerness to make himself a success. The move was a family one, his mother's people having relocated back south. She followed in an effort to improve Morgan's life. He was only thirteen and had already developed hoodlum behavior. He took to the local gangs and began ditching school to smoke marijuana with the group of bad hybrids he called friends.

In Memphis, around a better-behaved set of kids, Morgan's grades climbed gradually to A's and B's. Soon after, he aimed at one day being a college student. He would accomplish this by graduating from Memphis State University. Several years later, he returned to Chicago and received an advanced degree in political science. Thereafter, Morgan's career in local and state politics began. He was a favorite among his fellow Illinois government colleagues. And like many of them, he began to drink from the cup of corruption. The campaign contributions came in more often and with them so did the back scratches. His new taste for power kept his desire to remain in office alive. He adopted an attitude of doing whatever it took to keep his prominence and high profile in the public's eye. He would run and win a seat in the U.S. House of Representatives.

Then came the run for the Senate in which he pummeled his opponent by winning eighty percent of the votes. Senator Morgan was now one of the most powerful men in all of Washington. Now in line to make history as the first serious African-American Presidential candidate since Gary Lawson, a prominent theologian, Senator Morgan was no longer in control of his fate. Standing in his way to becomming the most power-ful man in the world was Pam Johnson, a no-name slut, who was the captain of his troubled tug at sea. She was a ruthless Jezebel, who was supposed to already be dead and out of the way.

Morgan regretted every moment he'd spent with her, but Pam made him feel in ways in which he hadn't before. It was her way of pushing him deeper into erotic pleasures that drove him crazy. Made him weak enough to allow the biggest mistake of his life. The careless moment when he allowed Pam to video-tape him. Her and the muscled stranger, who often participated in their sexual escapades, now haunted him. Morgan's wife knew of his bisexuality. A practice she'd thought was long gone after their marriage was consummated and his infidelity forgiven. Unfortunately, she was wrong!

# N a k e d      14

"Where's Eddie?" I asked in a moment of despair. "We haven't seen him since he left with us this morning."

"Wasn't he supposed to go to the police station," asked Karen.

"That's the last we've seen of him," replied Cedric.

"Us, too," said Charlotte.

"He don't know how to call nobody? Didn't his mamma teach him no better?" joked Tarnisha.

"Yes she did," said Eric. "Right after she said, 'Son, stop playing with dicks. And oh yeah, call home if you've been gone too long.'"

"*It* wasn't like that," I said. "*He* wasn't like that. I've known Eddie for a long time. And believe me, he was as much a man as you are, if not more. Still is, you ask me." I didn't really know where I was going with all of this. Truth be told, I didn't agree with Eddie's lifestyle either. In fact, it made me nauseous whenever I thought about it. But he was still a person. A man. A friend.

"You getting soft on me?" asked T.J. "I thought that was just for us artist types. Most cats think we're all a little fruity. Personally, I love women too much to ever think about going there. Never. Ever. You hear me? I'll be trying to tell cats, if you don't believe me, leave me alone with your girl. Them dudes won't do that 'cause they're scared."

"Soft," I insisted. "Soft? Soft has nothing to do with it. Eddie's still my friend, our friend. If he's in trouble, we've got to do something. Not sit around making judgments on who he's sleeping with. Only God can judge."

"Ain't nobody trying to judge," shouted Tarnisha. "I only joked about where the hell he was. Eric's the one who went there with all the gay jokes."

"Thanks, Tarnisha," mumbled Eric.

"The point is, there's no time for any of this," I said. "We have exactly five days left to find Pam and get this stuff straight, or we're going to be dead one way or another. I came here almost a week ago to get married. Then this all happened!" I was pointing at the box of folders resting on the edge of the counter without even realizing it.

"What about those," Karen asked. "Are we going to

open the rest of them?" She tried to reach into the box to grab one before I stopped her.

"There are only three names left," I said. And, unless we stop this, there will be more. That's if we're not dead first." I hoped that would be enough to stop any further inquiries and desires to open another folder. I was scared someone would find out something I didn't want them to know. I wanted to take my folder. In fact, I wanted to hide them all. It seemed like the only sensible thing to do. At this point, burning them would be the most sensible thing to do. I almost suggested it.

"We still have nothing to go on other than the information Special K. gave us tonight," I remarked. "He didn't know where Pam was, but he gave us enough to know what we need to do. And we can't leave until we do it. We have no clothes other than what we came here with for the wedding. And each of you has jobs and families. We cannot tell anyone, I mean anyone about this. The way I see it, anybody who knows anything will get caught up in this and who knows what will happen? I don't want that. And I don't think either of you do neither."

"I didn't say nothing," said Karen.

"Me, neither," said Tarnisha.

"Same here," added Cedric.

"Me, too," Charlotte said.

"You know me," T.J. said. "Out of sight, out of mind."

"I've covered me and Nicole," said Malik recalling an earlier call he'd to Memphis.

"I ain't said nothing," Eric said. "I'm away on business all of the time, anyway. I don't have a woman to run my mouth off to. I buys my pussy on the road. So I ain't got to put up with no shit!"

"Eric, you pay for pussy," asked Tarnisha. "I knew it! With that stank attitude of yours, I wondered how a woman would put up with you long enough to fuck you. You're always talking about getting laid. That's probably all you can get is the "paid for pussy."

"You're all whores one way or another."

"What!" Karen demanded. "You saying you see some ho's here?"

"Who the hell you calling a whore?" Charlotte challenged Eric to his face.

"Aw shit! Here we go." Cedric had seen this before.

"I ain't no damn whore!" shouted Tarnisha.

"Wait a minute, y'all," Eric said, trying to ease the tension he started. "I'm just saying women expect certain things from a man. You can't tell me money is not at the top of the list. Oh, you say all that other stuff like a charming personality, a gentleman, sensitive, attentive, faithful, go on. But, I've seen it all come down to the same thing: money. Whether it's buying dinner, paying for the movies, the house note or just straight saying, 'Baby, give me a couple hundred dollars for a little bit of this pussy. No strings attached! All the same thing. Whoring!"

"Negro, please," shouted Charlotte, who was now two inches from Eric's nose.

"Where's Shalamar?" I asked after separating the two before Eric got his ass whipped!

*  *  *

"What detective?"

"Stop it! You know who I'm talking about."

"Look. I don't know about…"

"You're a lie, Aunt Pam! Quit lying to me. Stop it. Since you convinced me to play this role for you, in order to get even with Jake, you've been lying to me. It's all a lie. I'm a lie. You're a lie. This whole thing is one big lie! And we're about to get killed for it!"

"Shut up! Now! I'm not about to let you spoil this. I told you what you needed to know."

"Told me, my ass! When you were shot, I was the one who took you to Mexico to get the surgeries you needed and still be safe. I'm the one who watched and took care of you for weeks until you could speak again. Then, before I could get a hug from you or you tell me you loved me, your first words were to ask me to help with this plot of yours. Begging me to betray someone, a friend, so you could get even with these people. I don't even know them and they've done nothing to me but show me love and kindness. That's more than I can say about you right now."

"I'm your damn flesh and blood, Shalamar."

"I don't know who you are anymore, since you had that damn plastic surgery and became this Jana person. I don't know who you are, Aunt Pam. I don't know who you are!"

"I had to do it! They were going to kill me if I stayed Pamela Johnson. I had to change my identity. Don't you understand that? They were going to kill me!"

"What do you want me to do? They've threatened to kill us, unless they get this videotape and some diary he keeps talking about."

"Stop it! Before someone hears you."

"They're all in the kitchen. Nobody can hear me."

# N a k e d 15

"Help! Uh...I did what you said. Help! Please! Somebody! I told them what you wanted me to."

Special K. held on to the wooden bridge as tightly as he could. His nails tore off as they dug into the wood of the old bridge he dangled from on the isolated farm land located about thirty miles outside of town near Gary. His life flashed before him. All the comedy shows, his wife, his promising future all now seemed in serious jeopardy. His fingers began to bleed. This time, his audience was hostile and there would be no laughing now.

"Thank you, Mr. K.," the goon in Hall's crew said. "We appreciate your cooperation. I'm afraid your services will no longer be needed."

"Please! Don't do this. Please! I'll do anything you want. I won't say nothing. Don't! Please! Help! Somebody help me please!"

"Oh, about the big break into show biz we arranged for you? We'll be sure to pass along your sincere regrets and that you had a change of heart and won't be going to California after all. Good-bye, Mr. Funny Man. Boys, drop him."

"No! Please! Please, help me! I'm begging you! Don't! No-o-o..."

His echo could be heard fainting as he fell towards the cold muddy water rushing underneath him. There was a loud splash. The mangled body and dreams of Kevin Robinson, better known as Special K., sank without a trace.

"I wonder what kind of audience the fish will make," joked one of the men in black suits.

"I don't know," said another. "I hope they find his shit funnier than I did."

"Come on," said the goon. "Let's get out of here."

"Gentlemen. Gentlemen. Settle down. Your work here is done. Let's move it." Detective Hall exited the vehicle he'd been sitting in while taking in the last minutes of Kevin's life.

"Mr. Hall? Is there anything else?"

"No," he replied. "Let's see what those other bastards come up with once they find out about this. Go! Get out of here with the others. I'll update him."

"The Senator?"

"Yeah, the Senator."

"What's next then?

"It's time to go deal with the other one!"

\* \* \*

"I'll be there tonight," confirmed Jana in a muffled whisper before looking over her shoulder to see if anyone heard her.

"Tonight? How will you find me? What do you want me to do, Aunt Pam?"

"I'll find you. Now shut up! Before somebody hears you."

"Nobody heard nothing!"

"I heard you!" Malik interjected from the doorway. He entered the room after spending the past few minutes with his ear at the edge of the closed door.

"It was nothing" lied Shalamar. She was trying to hide her tears after the interruption.

"I don't believe this shit!" shouted Pam from the other end.

"What are you talking about?" said Shalamar.

"What in the hell do you think I'm talking about?" corrected Malik. "I heard that shit. What the hell is going on? Who is that? Give me the damn phone!" Malik slammed the door behind him and moved towards Shalamar.

"Who is it?" demanded Jana. "Shalamar! Shalamar! Who's that? What's going on there?"

"Stop it!" screamed Shalamar, wrestling Malik for the

phone. "Stop! This has nothing to do with you."

"It does if you or whoever that is knows something about the diary and shit. Now give me the damn phone."

"Shalamar? Did they hear you? Shalamar?"

"Stop it! Let go of my wrist." The fight raged on for the phone.

"I'll be there tonight," Jana tried to reassure. "You've got to get away and meet me there at the spot we talked about. Tomorrow morning. Be there!"

"Who is this," asked Malik after he'd finally gotten control of the phone. "Who is this?" Only a dial tone greeted him.

"What's going on in here?" I questioned, after hearing the commotion from the kitchen. I went in to see what was up. "What is going on? Answer me!"

Indigo followed. "We heard you guys yelling all the way from the living room. Is everything okay?"

"Ask her," said Malik pointing at Shalamar.

Indigo and I were the only ones who went in to see what exactly was happening. Everybody else stayed and tried to calm the stuff about to jump off with Eric and Charlotte.

* * *

Shalamar reluctantly explained the plan her aunt devised to get revenge on me. The reason behind her burning desire to hate me so much and relentless pursuit to ruin my life was simple: I had ruined hers, so she thought. In her eyes, I was responsible for Kayra's death. It was my fault she fell in love with me and not her. If I would have left Kayra alone, maybe Detective Hall wouldn't have killed her, she thought. After the first night she and Kayra were together, Pam already decided to give Detective Hall and the Senator what they wanted. If Kayra had committed herself to Pam and only Pam, she would have protected her. Kayra's love was all Pam needed to get the shit she was involved in straight, and give up any evidence she had in her possession. Evidence which linked her and the Senator together.

Now, her plan was to get next to Indigo to get next to me. She'd use Shalamar for information to devise a master plan to end my marriage, career, and even my life.

"You only befriended me to help this bitch destroy my man," said Indigo, trying hard to keep her cool. "How could you do this to me? To my family? He's the father of my child. My soon-to-be husband. How could you do this shit to me? I cared for you like a sister."

"Was your affair with Ray all part of this, too," I asked. Trying to figure out how this sweet innocent looking girl had become the center of the affair that threatened our lives.

"No," she said with a bowed head. "He wasn't. That was a bizarre coincidence."

"Nothing has been a coincidence with you and your aunt. Nothing!" I shouted.

"Were you trying to ruin his life, too? Break up his marriage? Was that part of the grand plan, too? What did he do to you?" Indigo was ready to hit this poor soul, something totally out of her character.

"I swear," sobbed Shalamar. "I didn't know. I didn't know he was part of this."

"When is she coming?" I demanded.

"She will be here in the morning."

"And so will we," I added.

\* \* \*

Kevin's body disappeared into the lake. The next morning the killers returned to the basement of an old house somewhere on the West Side of the city and began torturing Eddie again. The beatings. The needles jabbed in his feet. The dry ice burning against his naked skin. It was all a medieval nightmare. He was bound around his ankles and wrists. When Detective Hall ordered them to stop, he watched Eddie bleed and scream. Then he made a call to the house. It was an offer of exchange. Eddie for the diary and the video.

His only chance to live was Jana. She'd flown into town in the middle of the night and waited at the spot she'd designated months ago. It was to be an asylum in case of trouble.

Fifty bucks to a willing fisherman, and we were in a boat next to Pam's secret spot, which was an abandoned boat docked on the Lake. His catches were light and the money we gave to rent his trawler for an hour or two was most welcome. Jana's boat was empty, and we had to wait for her arrival.

Indigo saw her first. I peered over the deck from where we were hidden to take a look for myself. I hadn't seen her in years. Her image was blurred. I blinked my eyes and took another look. I focused. It was a woman, but not a woman I'd seen before. Shalamar appeared next. The two women exchanged firm hugs. The woman with the unfamiliar face escorted Shalamar to the boat next to our rental. They walked quickly and disappeared. We followed closely behind.

*  *  *

Jana's love for her niece was strong. Much stronger than I'd thought could ever be imaginable for the stone cold, lying, deceitful, scandalous bitch I once knew. Everyone she loved died because of her. I was ready for it to end. It needed to end.

I watched for as long as could. The blood in my veins was beginning to boil. My hands were shaking and lips trembling. Then without notice, as involuntary as a heart beat, I felt my hand drop to my side resting on the steel which was tucked in my jeans underneath my shirt. Hiding. Waiting. I could hear my breath and felt my pupils narrowing from watching her. This shit was going to stop. The time had come, because every minute that went by raised the uncertainty and predictability quotient beyond tolerance. Then the involuntary motion continued and my clammy palm tightened around the handle with a nervous finger bending to fit inside the trigger guard. It all happened simultaneously with my arm raising straight out in front of me, solid and stiff like an erect penis.

Before the others could stop me, I ran as fast as I could to the woman. I reached her by surprise, holding the heavy piece of metal, pressing it tightly to her temple. The trigger cocked back. It felt cold. Just like death would, if it brushed up against you.

"Who in the fuck are you?!" I shouted.

I had tried to kill her Aunt. I don't know if I would have done it or not, but I wanted to. Badly.

The confrontation was an unexpected shock for Pam. It was Indigo, Malik, myself, and of course, Shalamar. We all watched as "Jana" lied her ass off and denied who she really was. Pam must have been a figment of my imagination, she said. The act had gone on long enough for Shalamar to realize time was running out and Pam wasn't going to reveal her true identity. She knew our lives rested on us getting to the bottom of this.

\* \* \*

I answered the phone and listened closely to the instructions Hall gave me. We were to be at the Pier at exactly one o'clock in the morning with the tape, the diary and Pam. No police. No tricks. He wanted Pam to make the drop. Eddie would be in another location waiting for us to pick him up once Hall gave his boys the signal.

Pam waited outside in an empty warehouse across from the Pier. She held the small duffle bag close to her body until she saw the two quick flashes of the headlights from a black sedan parked nearby that was her signal to move down towards the dumpster near the alley. She put the bag she carried inside the dumpster and picked up the black briefcase standing on end next to it. It was supposed to have close to a million dollars inside. It was a pay off in addition to Eddie's freedom.

In the shadows across the streets, she saw two silhouettes. She headed towards them, behind her the doors of the sedan quickly opened. Then two other cars screeched up from the alley. Pam hurried and began to run down the alley. It was dark. A figure moved into focus, another one came from behind. A hand grabbed her tightly about the arm. Before she could react to the firm grip, another man came from the other side of her, as the first set of shadows faded back into the darkness.

"Pam Johnson, we're with the Federal Bureau of Investigation. You're coming with us," said a pale white man with a proper high-pitched voice.

"For what? What's going on?"

"Conspiracy to commit murder."

"What? Who?"

Another agent rushed from a dark vehicle and demanded the attention of the man accosting Pam.

"Sir, Senator Morgan didn't make it. The bullet pierced his heart. He's dead."

"Make that murder! Cuff her and put her in the car." With a tight squeeze, he removed the briefcase from her hand.

"I didn't do anything, I swear! I didn't kill him. Why, I didn't even know him. I want my lawyer. Let go of me! Wait! Wait! They did it. They're the ones. They're upstairs. They were there. They killed him. Wait. I'll show you. They did it!"

"Save it for the judge and jury."

"But, I didn't do anything."

"What's this, then?"

There was no million dollars inside the briefcase. Instead, the agent found a disassembled high powered automatic rifle and a silencer.

* * *

Eddie was calm given the fact he'd spent the past forty-eight hours locked in a basement, naked, and tortured. We found him staggering around the corner with only a filthy blanket he found in the garbage.

"You've got to stop them," he whispered stumbling into my arms. "They're going to kill us."

"Come on," I said. "Let's find Pam and get the hell out of here!" I couldn't believe I was concerned about a woman who'd tried ruining my life.

We drove the block and a half between the two drop-off

points like we were instructed. When we got to the corner I dimmed the headlights and crept along at a low speed to the abandoned warehouse. From the front gates we could see Pam being hustled into a long black sedan. I stopped.

"Damn," I said. "They got her. She must have made the drop. That's why they let you go, Eddie. Hell, if they were going to kill us, they would've done it by now." It didn't matter though. I was still scared as hell and so were the others.

"I've got an idea," I said. "We're going to give those bastards a taste of their own medicine. But first, we've got to get out of here before we get caught, too."

I turned us around and sped away. I asked Eddie if he needed us to take him to a hospital. He said 'no,' and we went to the only base we had, his house. Pops was worried. Very worried, and it showed. He had gotten word from a friend at the station, who'd warned that these were some bad asses we were dealing with. They were going to pin Senator Morgan's murder on Pam, and they needed to get us to cover their tracks.

The department's Internal Affairs Unit had been watching Hall for a while. But everybody seemed too scared to pin a case on him. Eddie was Pop's only kid and he loved him very much. I felt sorry for him having to sit there and wait to find out if his son was still alive or not. After we'd gotten Eddie cleaned up and rested, Pops was able to tell us just enough for me to come up with a plan. It was to begin the next morning.

\* \* \*

We met Butter at K.'s dressing room. He was still in shock about his friend's murder. We could tell by the dark rings under his eyes and the blank look he kept on his face. He told us where Detective Hall's hidden office was. It was a location kept very private for obvious reasons. There, he'd made secret deals with almost every dignitary in the state. My idea was simple; tape one of the meetings and get him by the balls like he had us for the past week. Besides, we knew it was only a matter of time before he would try to kill us again.

\* \* \*

Malik and I found the office the next night and we managed to bug the place. Later there was a meeting, just like Pops said there would be when he met with another one of his informants at the station.

After the meeting we went back to the office and gathered the evidence we needed. Then, we made a call of our own, like the many we had gotten from Hall. We threatened to expose his ass, if he didn't find a way to delete and seal for good, whatever files he had on us.

The next day an FBI agent paid us a visit and handed us a reeled tape and a sealed envelope with several strips of micro-fiche film. On them was the very essence of our lives, right there on film, taken by people who we didn't know, but who knew us beyond that of an intimate friend. He told us they have these documents on everybody and we were one of the extreme lucky ones, who ever got a chance to get their lives back. He warned we would have to forever watch our backs very carefully, considering how close we had come to being involved in one of the biggest sex scandals in recent political history. And one day it might all come to haunt us! However, he assured us for now we were safe.

It comforted us Hall wouldn't be coming after us again no time soon. He was really one of them, the agent informed us. Hall was actually working undercover for the FBI. His tactics and behavior, though, were way out of control, the agent agreed. He said, they needed Hall because of his contacts and ties to the underground crime world. He was like an independent contrator. I knew they knew about all the people he killed and the Feds went on record as not condoning his actions. The agent didn't say it, but we figured everything out. The Senator had been the real target all along. They used all the years of Pam's history with him against her. She was the perfect candidate to take the wrap for his murder. And, although she wasn't directly involved, there was enough evidence tied to her to put her away for life! There was nothing we could do about that.

The next morning we made a stop to the Attorney General's office. I left the evidence with his secretary after giving her instructions and walked out. At least, maybe, it would help to guarantee our safety.

# N a k e d   16

t was eleven o'clock in the morning and T.J. lit his first joint. He was sitting in his study room looking at the shelves of books he collected. Most were written by black authors, who wrote contemporary African-American fiction. Though he would pick up a white author or two from time to time such as John Grisham, John Irving or his favorite, J.F. Freedman.

Then his cell phone rang. It was the gallery, which a month earlier had deemed his painting pornographic and had no place with the rest of their collection.

Two of the featured artists had canceled for a big upcoming showing. One, because of a scheduling conflict, and the other due to sudden illness. The gallery already had one artist on standby in case of such an emergency, but they were unprepared for two. T.J.'s work, as shocking as they proclaimed it to be, were the only pieces they've seen, which possessed the quality they needed for the showing. The curator was forced to eat crow and apologize for the gallery's narrow-mindedness. T.J.'s paintings were finally displayed in the gallery's big event and were an instant hit.

Reflecting on it all, T.J. smiled. The sticky green weed felt good as he inhaled the smoke of redemption. It was his way of relaxing. Letting it all go.

\* \* \*

One Saturday, on a warm mid-summer day, Charlotte laughed at herself for the first time in a long time. Before we came to town and started that nightmare last Fall. She had spent the last six years fighting legal cases, to keep her company from bellying up from the mounds of lawsuits stemming from one thing or another. All to the neglect of her family and herself. The stress made her hardnosed and angry.

Monday she returned to her job with her resignation in hand, along with a decision to take her practice elsewhere, or even to do something different altogether. She'd always wanted to write.

\* \* \*

Eric made it back to Cincinnati. Waiting for him one day from a long business trip was the only woman who came close to gaining his affections and his heart. She was a short, petite young woman with plenty of sex appeal. Her career was her focus and paid her generously. There were no children, but her free time as rare as it was, was well spent remodeling her spacious home.

Eric arrived at the airport late. He had been gone a week and she missed him a lot. The lovely woman showed him just how much when she entered the terminal wearing a long satin coat and nothing else but shoes with a big smile.

She and Eric held their affections long enough to find an empty women's restroom. There the woman untied the tightly drawn belt that held together the coat she wore. She slowly opened it to reveal her smooth tanned skin. Her nipples stood firmly. They were hardened by the thoughts of Eric's long dick deep inside her. He opened his shirt, unzipped his pants and moved towards her. He wrapped his hands around her small waist and put his lips on her left nipple. She squirmed at the soft touch. When he turned and kissed her right nipple she grabbed his head.

Her pussy was wet and she couldn't wait to feel him. Eric lifted her onto the sink. It's cold. She doesn't notice. Her head leans back and her legs instantly part. His tongue goes down the center of her shivering body. Between her breast. Then to her navel. He began to feel the soft hairs brush against his chin, lips, and nose. The hairs laid flat as his moist tongue dampened them until he came down over her horizon and the tip of his tongue gently touched her clit. Her toes curled and fingers straightened. She jumped, grabbing his head tighter. He feels her fingernails planted in his skull. Ignoring the pain, he moves his tongue slowly around her solid target before placing his soft lips to hers, taking them slightly inside his mouth. She could feel his warm breath floating inside her and surrounded his neck with her thighs. He stayed there until she came.

He was now fully erect and moved the head of his nine-inch manhood against her swollen lips, easing himself inside of her. She moaned with every inch she felt. They clinched each other as tightly as possible. He moaned with each dip he took. Her hips moved with his. She turned around. And he entered her from behind. His thrusts were faster. Stronger.

He grabbed her hair hard enough to make her head go back. Then he held the back of her neck. She moved faster and became wetter than before. He moved faster and got harder. Their tensed passion met and they each let out a well-earned grunt. "Ahhh," they exhaled together. Before they could rest, the door opened and there were voices. Eric and the woman quickly pulled themselves inside a stall and slammed the door behind them. It was a good fifteen minutes before the coast was clear.

* * *

Tarnisha decided to take an extra week off from her pharmaceutical sales job. As much smart-mouth talking she did, the past few months had really shaken her up. At home she turned the ringer off of the phones and refused to answer the door for visitors. Her guy friends would just have to understand. Dating was a chore anyway, she thought. Time to herself was what she wanted and needed. She thought about calling Eric. Despite the circumstances, they seemed to hit it off the last night in Chicago and he expressed interest in seeing her again. "But why put up with his bullshit," she asked herself. "He'll end up being filed under *came and went*, anyway," she thought.

\* \* \*

Eddie recovered from the broken bones and bruises he got from the ass kicking Hall's guys gave him. We keep in touch regularly now and have gotten our friendship back on track. Last time we talked, he told me he has a new lover. Someone he met at T.J.'s art showing. He seemed to be happy with his life. I'm sure he was even happier now that we had gone. I can't say I agreed with his lifestyle but hey, he's still cool with me and I'll be praying for him.

Oh and Pops, he finally got control of his constipation problem and was last seen dancing the night away at *The Blue Bird*. I hope he stays out of trouble. It can get wild in that place!

\* \* \*

That bitch Pam got what she deserved! She was sentenced to twenty years to life and is serving time at a federal women's prison in upstate New York. For all she'd done to fuck up every-body's life, I was glad to finally have her out of mine for good! At an all women's prison, I was sure she'd do enough fishing to occupy her time, if you know what I mean.

Shalamar still manages to visit her aunt from time to time. I guess she couldn't completely turn her back on her despite all she'd done. She never finished her internship with Indigo, but my wife is a forgiving woman and they still keep in touch. Maybe one day, they can be friends again. And believe it or not, Shalamar and T.J. hooked up. The last I heard, she was planning another trip back to Chicago. Knowing T.J., I hope she packs light.

* * *

Rachel and Ray. What can I say? They stayed together. It wasn't easy, though. She and Ray were able to put the whole thing behind them and move on with their lives, once Rachel was able to forgive Ray and Ray found Jesus. He learned a lesson we all should, I guess there's a little Maynard in all of us.

* * *

Me? Well, very simple. Indigo and I had our wedding. It was a quiet ceremony at a small chapel in the country. There were no outside guests. No friends. No planning. No shit. Railey was there to give Indigo away. And the reverend's wife stood as a witness.

When we left Chicago and got back to New York, we resisted the temptation to make love before our wedding night. At least, the last week anyway. It was a short time to go without sex, or so we thought. Every day was a struggle. When our wedding night finally came, every moment of resistance was worth it. The lovemaking was slow and passionate. The room was filled with candles and my wife gave me every essence of her womanly being. Her spirit engulfed me. We started on the bed. She held the canopy post as she rode me to ecstasy. I later held her underneath me and slowly moved in an easy, circular motion, as I whispered in her ear all the beautiful things I loved so much about her. She whispered back to me between her cries of pleasure. I let go of all my emotions. All I was as a man came with me. All that she was as a woman came with her. We became as one despite the nakedness of having our souls exposed.

# EPILOGUE

n the wee hours after Indigo was asleep, I became restless and quietly eased out of bed, tipping across the room. I was still butt naked and the hardwood floors felt cold against my bare feet. When I got to the dresser, I scrambled for a pair of warm-ups and a sweatshirt, being careful not to make any loud noises. Then I went for a walk. The night was quiet and still. I looked up at the sky, which was clear with a bright moon surrounded by plenty of stars.

After getting to the end of our long street, passing the huge lots of the few houses in the neighborhood. My steps were slow but steady. There were no lights on and no eyes watching. It felt good! Then, before I could completely enjoy the moment, as I approached the next block, I heard the loud screech of tires from behind me. I turned and could see the bright headlights turning the corner. I began to walk faster. The car slowed to a creep. I could feel the lights burning brightly against my back. I walked even faster. Then faster. My muscles tensed as I prepared to run. Then the lights turned to darkness as the car made a right into the entrance of one of the estates and disappeared in the long driveway leaving me be.

At home, my muscles relaxed and I let out a big sigh of relief. I looked up at the star filled sky and the words, "Thank you God," was all I could manage to say.

EXCERPT
FROM THE UPCOMING RELEASE

*Love Letters on the Wall, the blues for Nia*
a novel

## ALL ABOARD!  ALL ABOARD!

## MAKE YOUR DREAMS OF LOVE COME TRUE

*Congratulations! You have been chosen to attend a truly magnificent event.*

The first ever cruise to the island paradise of EDEN! Yes, you've read correctly. We have arranged an all expense trip *(with the exception of a small $200.00   donation for historical purposes)* to the *Garden of Eden! Yes, the actual garden paradise island* with a special bonus added. A guided tour to *"The Wall of  Nia."*  Legend has documented, that it's engraved love letters from 18th century lovers will put the love back into any fallen relationship.

      This could be your last chance to see if there's any hope. Won't you just come! Your cruise ship will be the legendary, *Dream of Dreams*. Our motto *"We make miracle happens!"*

OKAY, you're still not convinced? We'll make a money back gurant.........

*My little honey dip of hip*
*Sunshine Divine*
*You confused my mind*
*Before I knew*
*I had the blues for you*

# Chapter 1

ɱɛʟʟoɯ. ʂɱooʈɦ. The midnight hour was as calm as a woman with flowers in her hair. The night rainfall had stop. A cool gentle breeze slowly nudged the lingering clouds exposing the full silver moon. The city had long been given the nickname, "City of Lights." Tonight the floodlights shining on the many magnificent palaces and monuments of the skyline seamed more brilliant. Boats filled The Seine River delivering night goers to the right and left banks of the city. The Champs de Mars rumbled with patrons eating and drinking into the wee hours. The rhythm could easily be felt.

Stachel "Stach" Wilson stood quiet. Still as he possibly could. The breeze slightly caressed his skin with each past it made. He closed his eyes, titled his head back and inhaled deeply. When he no longer felt the touch of the breeze, he exhaled to fee his thoughts. Clear his mind.

He reflected on his passion for music. Jazz. The saxophone. Indeed, Stach was a jazzman. He stood six feet tall with long slender hands and fingers. On his head was short cropped hair and face a goatee connecting to a thin mustache.

3

He never cared much for fancy clothes. Instead, he leaned more toward an arty, renaissance look. Unmistakably, he would have looked the part of a jazzman whether he liked it or not.

Growing up in lower Manhattan, he found himself surrounded by perils he didn't want to succumb to. The neighborhood of the two-story brownstone flat he lived and played as a child, beneath corruption. Mobster's pranced and hung about in fine clothes. Pinned striped suits mostly. Their timepieces tangled from their vests. They enforced their own unlawful rules by using strong armed tactics. Sometimes leaving mutilated corpses openly in nearby playgrounds for young kids to see. Runners hurriedly raced through the neighborhoods. Delivering cases of prohibited alcohol to those bold enough to challenge the system. Even more tempting, were the beautiful syphilis stricken strumpets. Stach feared he might one day accept one their invitations and catch the deadly disease.

He tried not to allow himself to be entrapped by these and many other fates. With the encouragement of his father, Stach turned to music. Although his father had fallen victim to his own constant drunkenness and had many other shortcomings, he still managed to offer sober advice and concern for Stach's future. His father prayed his love would rescue him from the same self-destruction he had suffered.

Stach remembered one particular hotter than July day, in the middle of the month of May. His father came home from work, or whatever he mysteriously did to sustain his family from poverty and destitution. In his large sweaty hands, were two tickets to the opening of Duke Ellington's Jazz Band All-stars at Harlem's Cotton Club. How he came about obtaining them was anybody's guess. Stach's mother had some suspicions—none of which comforted her. However, the gesture to introduce her son to society's other side, full of the 1927 style of exuberance and jubilation, was indeed noble and genuine. Therefore, it went without challenge.

That night still shined vividly in his mind. The dance hall filled with laughter, back rooms clouded with smoke, the beautiful bodies jigging on air with energy and grace. The music offered sounds that brought life to the mind, body and soul. In many cases, could be felt long after the party ended. He and his father communicated in a way they never had before. Just the way, Stach was sure his father had planned. He discovered jazz. And although he was only sixteen, it was the night he became a jazzman!

* * *

When Stach opened his eyes again, the gleaming beauty of Paris was now in full view. He had been here before. A decade ago while he was still in the Army. He loved Paris and it loved him.

This occasion was different though. It had been a little more than six months ago when the brochure came in the mail. Sent special deliver, notifying him that he and several others were invited on this cruise to paradise. The invitation was convincing. A free flight to Paris. Seven days cruising the Atlantic to Africa. A visit to paradise, *the Garden of Eden*, if there was such a place. Why they were selected they did not know. But it was a chance to escape. Make a last effort to work the kinks out.

The only information each member was provided was that the selection was based almost solely on the nature of their relationships with their mates. No criteria was given, but certainly these were not just random choices. Maybe, they all needed something that was missing. Something each desperately needed. A spark. Even a flame if needed. The voids

5

ran deep. Easily masked. Nevertheless, still there. If flying to Paris, a city which bleed romance, going to an island paradise and reading love letters on a wall named *Nia* was the answer, then they all were willing to risk it. Especially, the visit to *Nia*. Her magic was said to be powerful. The magical love letters written upon her surface able to heal inwardly. The recipients of the invitations knew not how much truth rested in these expectations. But to do nothing meant certain failure and heartbreak.

Those who were asked to come came. From all over they came. Australia, Canada, East and West Coast's of the United States and many other places. They entered the airport from their varies locations in an unified effort to find love, once and for all. Keep it. Stay there. Make a sad, happy. A low, high. A bad, good. They all came.

* * *

Here they met tonight. Midnight July 14, 1951, at the port Le Havre in Paris, France onboard the *Dream of Dreams*. It was finally allowed at sea again. After being christened in 1928, the ship didn't actually set sail until 1935 because of reported mechanical difficulties. Others rumored tells that the ship was haunted and reported several strange deaths aboard her decks. Which ever was true, she was a mighty warrior. It had sailed during World War I in the Red Sea. Although only a passenger vessel she withstood several attacks by enemy fire. With each return back home to port, successfully delivering her crew to sea, she showed why she had earned the name she bore. Her Captain, Samuel Mackenzie became an unsung hero of the war. His six successful transcontinental journeys amidst enemy territory made him a highly respected officer in the Naval Fleet.

It also earned him the nickname he received for his accomplishments. More than that, it represented a constant reminder of the events of that last historic trip which changed Six's life forever.

That night he had sailed into torrid seas and heavy thunderstorms. The seas grew and continued to produce high waves and with the thunderstorms pouring down, visibility became difficult at best. As he crossed hostile territory, his ship received rapid enemy fire. Captain Mackenzie maneuvered quickly avoiding some of the hits. The attack continued and he again tried to turn sharply. This time the ship became unstable, throwing two members of the crew overboard. Negro men. They were on deck securing the hatches when it happened. To rescue them Mackenzie ordered the ship's Helmsman to beak off their maneuvers, leaving the ship vulnerable for attack.

The Captain and three other crewmen were able to extend floaters attached to thick ropes. As they pulled them aboard, the ship took a direct hit to her broad side. Killing thirteen other crewmen. White men. Moments afterwards, the colored men were brought up to safety. Mackenzie quickly ordered the maneuvers started again, to avoid any further damage. But not before the lives of the other men had been sacrificed. By night's end, the ship eventually found port. She was shaken but not destroyed.

Three months later, the Navy turned its back on one of its own. The twenty-two years of dedicated service and heroic missions were forgotten. They forced Captain Mackenzie to retire or face court-martial proceedings for unnecessarily jeopardizing the lives of his crew. In effect, they said he was responsible for the deaths of those thirteen he lost. The lost of white lives to save those of the colored, was unacceptable and

7

unforgivable. There would be no medals. No gratitude. No honor.

Eleven years later, Six was again captain of the vessel he once sailed. It had become apart of the Navy's aging fleet and was auctioned to an old shipyard, which Six worked. He talked the owner into refurbishing the ship again as an vacation cruise liner. His desire and passion was apparent. Now tonight the *Dream of Dreams* would set sail again for the first time in over a decade.

# Chapter 2

chanel parker was a stage performer in Paris some years ago. Her voice chimed like with the grace of a bird singing. Her aunt and uncle had raised her in Paris and were her adopted parents. After her own were killed at the hands of a mercenary, during a terrorist attack at a political convention. Her father, a black political leader, had met her French mother when they were both students at the University of Chicago.

When they were killed, her mother's sister, adopted Chanel immediately. She was an only child and Chanel had already visited her on many occasions in Paris. She was ten at the time they took her as their daughter. The acceptance of a Negro girl being raised by a French family was slow. But with time she survived. More than survived. She became Paris and it her. She marveled at the culture and the character of the city. Her family ensured the little girl's behavior and etiquette were at its best. More importantly, inside her soul still remained her parent's lessons of the love of God, dignity, honesty and respect.

When she became a woman at nineteen, she decided
to pursue her dream of coming to America again and becoming
an American fashion model. Many wanted her obvious physical
beauty for profit. Her body was perfectly proportioned. Her
long, long legs made her stilt above most men of average
height. Straight coal black hair rested on her shoulders
resembled a black silk curtain. Her breast were slightly under
the size to be considered large, but nevertheless stood round
and firm. They were made distinctively noticeable by her flat
sunken stomach, small waist and the narrow hips of her tall
slender body. Her smooth fair skin made her ethnicity difficult
to identify. A fact she despised wholeheartedly, but used to her
advantage fully. She was proud to be a Negro woman.

She eventually made it to America. New York. After
only a few months her dreams faltered. Men entered her life for
the first time. And after a brief relationship with Negro solider,
she became impregnated with a child. Married, he fled into
obscurity and she remained alone, leaving her little choice but to
return to Paris. She had a daughter of her own. A lovely one.
She had all the characteristics of her mother. They grew
together, mother and child.

When Chanel turned twenty-six, new dreams wore deep
within her soul. Singing became her pursuit. It was a natural gift
she received from her mother, who had her own aspirations of
singing and dancing her way to stardom. This dream Chanel did
fulfill. She became a local favorite as a blues singer. She sung
the blues because it felt closes to her. Rhythmic. Soulful. She
sung it with the passion and truth it deserved.

One day while she performing at a local tavern, in
walked a handsome, tall man. He looked comfortable and
familiar. He was a player. She could tell, before she ever saw

the worn black case, which held his instrument. Saxophone, She had seen him playing around town. She had even sat in on one of his sets once before, after one of her own performances. His music fascinated her, although he didn't play professionally and was only an enthusiast. Tonight their eyes connected and before either knew it, he had taken his instrument out and was performing with her. They made love to the music they played. His jazzy sound was a perfect fit with her blues vocals.

By night's end he couldn't resist the intriguing young woman. The night held 'til morning. They had become inseparable. Now three years later with plans of marriage, their relationship had suffered. The tighter they held on, the further they grew apart. This trip would be a certain test of their love.

* * *

Most of the other ship's other passengers brought with them an enormous amount baggage in their lives. Each moment that quickly went by, proved to be filled with revelations.

Flower Evans, the twenty-four year old daughter of Six Mackenzie. He had invited her to accompany him on the cruise to ease her crushed heart after a recent irreconcilable breakup with her fiancée of one year. After their estrangement, Flower became extremely promiscuous. Her father's suspicions of her elide affairs were confirmed, when three weeks ago he returned home early from a short port run. He walked in to discover their neighbor's seventeen year old son's face planted deep between Flower's thighs. Her legs were straddled upon his shoulders, as she tightly griped his head. How lucky the boy had been Six thought, that his twelve and a half boot had gotten caught in the glass table he barreled over, giving the lad just a hair enough room to rush screaming out the door unclothed. While she blamed her actions on the stress of her breakup.

* * *

Then there was York Mendell. A short, thin Australian fellow with long sandy hair and a slight reddish tan. He was raised in a very modest middle class family back in the land downunder. Life was simple on the farm he spent his childhood and most of his adult life. When he was thirty-two working as a hired hand with his father, his grandfather died. Leaving him a share of the millions he earned from livestock investments. His grandfather in his wisdom resisted the allurement of announcing his fortune and kept his secret discreetly from everyone. Despite the constant rumors. Instead, he was content seeing York, his father, and mother working diligently together on the farm without all of the distractions and hassles he knew would come. He figured once he was dead, he'll leave them his life's earning and explain his decision in his will, which he did.

When the family received the inheritance, just as York's grandfather had predicted, things changed quite a bit for the worse. York's relationship with his father, which had always been close, now was strained by York's father attempt to cut him out of his share of the money. In fact, it wasn't long before York's parents started feuding over how the money should be spend or saved. York's mother was happy with the quality of life they were living. They made a few relatively small purchases, such as new farm equipment, and remodeling for the house. The rest of the money she was content to put into savings for a rainy day. Although, it would have taken a lot of rain to go through the eleven and a half million dollars. York's father wanted to abandon the farm and made some risky

12

financial investments with a neighbor. Both were unacceptable ideas to his wife.

After several months of continued augments over the superfluous manner in which his father started to live, his wife felt their marriage going down the drain like a pulled plug. Eventually, the farm was sold after his father's refusal to work it any longer, leaving the ground unattended with exception of the little work York and his mother could do by themselves.

He convinced York's mother to move to the United States. California, where a millionaire should be, he thought. York however, wasn't fond of the idea of leaving his homeland so quickly. Reluctantly, York's father agreed to give him one million dollars to stay or do with as he pleased. York remained in Australia and deposited his money in a bank account, making withdrawals only to pay for his boarding room and other living expenses. After ten years he visited California only once. To comfort his mother after his father ran off with a large breasted, blonde film star, who smelled the money all over him.

Now he was quickly becoming an aging middle aged forty-two year old man, York decided it was time for a change. With ten years of compounding interest earning on his money, York found he had acquired an astounding fortune that dwarf his initial million-dollar deposit. He realized it was time to experience a whole lot more. He heard much about New York City. Since it shared the same the name as he, York decided it would be there he would start his new life with his "new" money.

* * *

Lisa Hillsbury, had come from the Midwest, after finishing her education at the University of Kansas, were she vigorously pursued her bachelor's degree in education. She had further ambitions of obtaining a doctorate, and becoming the Nation's first female school superintendent. Midway through her graduate studies, she fell in love with a fellow student. He was also in his first year of the master's program. They fell in love and soon married. Two years later, while returning home from a party, her and her husband were involved in a horrible car cash. A drunken driver had ran them uncontrollably off the road. Their vehicle flipped down the steep hill, which ran along the curved shoulder of the highway. The rescue attempt took four hours and prove to be fatal for Lisa's husband and left her with severe internal injuries and unable to have children.

After spending two months in the hospital recovering from her injuries, she no longer had the zest and determination she once did. The tragedy made it difficult for her to remain in Kansas. With her recent thirty-sixth birthday, she felt her life was turning into a downward spiral. No husband, no children, no more dreams for the future.

In a last effort for survival, she moved to Los Angeles with her older sister Kelley, who had invited her there as an opportunity to start over. There she settled on an elementary school teacher's position. Nothing fancy, no expectations, just a job. Being around the children in some strange way helped her come to the realization she wouldn't be having any of her own. In fact, she doubted her ability to even get another man now that show walked with a noticeable limp and now had a large scare that rested on her face. It ran from her right nostril, under her cheek and ended at the corner of her jawbone. Her disfigurements harden her in ways she wasn't proud. Her once very attractive face, turn to what Lisa herself deemed appalling and she developed a personal vendetta against the world. Men in particular, as if they were responsible for her misfortune.

# Chapter 3

    **"All Aboard! All Aboard!** It's time for *The Dream of Dreams* to begin the journey to paradise. Destination. Eden. All Aboard! All Aboard! The destine of a war filled life could be heard in his voice. He was an enormous man in both stature and weight. The sound of his loud imprudent cry rode the warm gentle breeze that surrounded the peaceful midnight hour. His gray bearded face sported a small crease in the corner of his thin lips. Holding back an inevitable smile, which was trying to escape. The passion in his voice could be felt down to the marrow of their bones, as he gave one final roar to those who had been chosen to board *The Dream of Dreams*. This time none would answer the call.

    Stach and Chanel stood leaning against the massively rope that lined the thick bright red rails surrounding the deck. Their knuckles grew white from grasping it tightly, as to not risk becoming nameless casualties swallowed into the depths of the sea. Without any further notice, the Captain raised his long arm, breaking the crease of his heavily starched blue uniform, with it's embroidered gold seams and large brass buttons.

He slowly began walking up the long ramp of the awaiting ship. His dark piercing eyes momentarily stopped their probing and focused for an eternity, or so it seemed, at the couple looking down at him from above. They tried as hard as they could to look away but their pupils grew larger as his pinned. Soon a cremating heat rushed through their bodies like a river run wild. The night reeked of eerieness. Finally, his eyes released them. The blood in their veins settled like a pot of boiling water on stove that had just been turned off. The visions of the star filled galaxy could be seen again, bouncing reflections of lights off the pulchritudinous seas.

The ship's boiler-room crew filled with large unsightly men was hot. Very hot. They began the sequence of shoveling coal into the furnace to satisfy the ship's massive appetite for fuel. Each man sweated profusely, as they went about their duties to create enough burning energy required to move the 209-foot vessel. Finally, when just enough power ran throughout the engine the loud whistle blew indicating the ship's movement and departure from the port.

Stach and Chanel unclenched the rope and shook their hands frantically to regain the feeling in them and calm the unbearable tingling. They turned to find the doors leading inside to the main quarters as the numbness slowly went away. They could feel the crushed brochure they still held. Too afraid to speak, they simultaneously looked and read again the advertisement that lured them here. As if to say to each other, "What in the hell have we gotten ourselves into!"

* * *

Stach reached in his left shirt pocket to find the wrinkled boarding pass given to them upon their arrival at the departing gate. "There here we go, lower deck three, section E, cabin 13A."

"It would be 13," she commented, perturb that with all things considered they were assigned to that particular cabin. They walked cautiously towards the bow of the ship finding the stairs leading down to the main accommodation floor. Once downstairs, they entered a narrow hallway not much bigger than the width of a door and required turning sideways to pass if anyone approached.

"Damn. Where is everybody?" he mumbled as he led her down the nearly dark corridor some twenty-five feet. The only illumination came from a single flickering bulb hanging some additional feet ahead. Revealing what appeared to be the silhouette of a passenger standing in front of another faintly seen doorway. "Hello. Is there anyone there?" Stach weakly cried.

Chanel held him firmly as they began to walk swiftly towards the shadowy figure, who offered no response to their greeting. As they got close, the ship rumbled with great force, shaking and bouncing them against the deck walls. The floor beneath them felt as if it had collapsed. The light once again blinked off, as it too swung fiercely by its cord.

"Oh my God!" cried Chanel. The force threw her to the ground as she desperately tried to hold onto his hand.

"No!" he yelled, as he too buckled and fell on top of her. Then as quickly as it all began it stopped. The ship stood calm and a final blink lifted darkness. They tightly held each other. "Darling are you alright?" he asked trying to gather himself while also providing a comforting touch against her cheek.

"Whew! What was that?" she sighed. She rubbed her head to exam a possible injury. "Yes, I guess I'm okay." she resultantly answered as they supported each other to stand. They stood leaning against the wall bracing for another eruption, if there were to be one. None happened.

"It's beyond me what's going on, but it's time to find out. Look!" he demanded, pointing towards the doorway near the light where the figure earlier stood. "He's gone!"

"Please Stach, let's leave. NOW!" The idea of finding him seemed trivial. They had been onboard the *Dream of Dreams* not much pass an hour, and all had been a nightmare. There were no signs of any other occupants on the vessel, only that of the silent shadow near the door who couldn't be seen anymore.

This time instead of a swift walk, Stach and Chanel ran as quickly they humanly could towards the door. He reached for the knob. The door burst opened before his long hands could grasp the handle. Startled, they jumped and froze in fear. The darkness was suddenly replaced by a bright florescence light, which momentarily blinded the couple. Their eyes were sensitive from the long period void of light. At the entrance stood a large bearded man sporting a familiar ensemble. The brass buttons on his sharply pressed uniform seemed even more brilliant then before as they reflected off the light.

"Well look adhere. Ooh. Ooh." he laughed with his deep baritone voice. We've been looking for you two." He laughed once more as he looked at them with amusement. "You can close your mouths now. I'm not going to hurt you." His vocalization trembled through the air.

"Huh? What? Who are you?" insisted Stach, slowly moving Chanel behind him to protect her. "Wait a minute. I've seen you before. Aren't you the steward we saw shortly after we boarded, just before we set sail?"

"Six. Six Mackenzie, your ship's Keeper. That means I'm a little bit of everything including the Captain. To you I'm God while you're own my ship. Don't ever forget that!" His deep raspy voice rang powerful and true. The thick grayed eyebrows resting on his hog head curled upward and extended slightly pass his face. He looked at them stroking his grayed beard with the palm of his wide hand. The warning was clear. His point made.

"And just so you know, I usually just supervise and let my Helmsman do most of the work. I prefer to mingle with my passengers. Besides, we have a porter who we call Cap. A young colored boy I found stored away on my ship after we left port from a test run. He was abandoned by his family. For what reason he never said. Probably, because he's slow upstairs, if you know what I mean. I'll keep him around anyway, as long as he does a little work, stay out of sight, and out of the way."

"That's touching. It really is. "Where are we? How do we get out of here to get to our room? And where are the other guests? We've been on this ship for over an hour and we haven't seen one single solitary soul."

Chanel eased herself from behind him to better her view at the man who had suddenly entered. Her long summer tan dress was wrinkled from her fall and loosely twisted around her tall slim figure. The right strap laid helplessly down her shoulder. The brown leather sandals she wore flopped about her feet, as she maneuvered to get them back on without bending. Keeping her eyes centered on the ego tripped man who had all but demanded he be shown reverence. "Sir, Six or whatever. What is going on? We came down here looking for our cabin and somehow we ended up in this dark cave. This was suppose to be a pleasure cruise and so far it's been hell!" Her voice

19

increasingly gained more courage, as her struggle with her sandal ended and she completely emerged into view.

She lifted her strap onto her shoulder and twisted her dress back into its proper position. "I had reservations about coming on this thing anyway. Whatever problems we are having in our relationship, we could have worked them out some other way. " Her hands fell upon her curved hips. "I've been scared almost from the moment we set foot on this *Dream of Dreams* boat of yours. Which is a bunch of bullsh...."

"Chanel!" shouted Stach interjecting before more got said to make matters worse. "Look, my fiancée is just upset right now. We've been through a lot in such a short time. Can you please show us to our cabin and help us find the others?"

"Hold it right there son. You got a feisty colored girl there. You ought try keeping better control of her." Stach frowned at the words he spoke, but kept his tongue despite the anger felt raising within him. "Let's get this clear. I'm not the one who went through the wrong door and rushed down here. The door on the left leads to this containment area you're in at the moment. "You and this, this." He stopped what he was about to say after he saw the displeasure on their faces not to mention the rage he noticed building on the face of Stach. "The door on the right leads upstairs to the floor, just above here where you and the other folks will be staying. So get your things and let's go. I believe most of them are already in the banquet room already getting aquatinted. Unless you rather just stay here." he laughed hauntingly and hit Stach stiffly on the shoulder. "Come on boy and colored, I'm mean..Ms..follow me."

"My name is Chanel. Chanel Parker. And I certainly would appreciate if that's who you acknowledge me as." She looked calmly at him. Then reached for her black oversized leather purse crumbled in the corner of the doorway. She had dropped it during the moment of Six's grand entrance.

"A fancy and proper one of them I see. I know who you are. I personally invited both of you. Surprised? Good! Come on and follow me." He held the door with surprised courtesy and then led them up two flights of stairs, to the corridor leading to another hatch. As Six opened the enormous thick metal block, sounds of laughter rushed from its seams.

Once fully opened, exposed was a large dinning room full of gathered passenger who also had been invited on the historic journey. All of them seemed at ease and noticeably in good cheer. Stach and his bride to be, looked at each other dumfoundly. Their worries and concerns melted away as they looked upon the joy on everyone faces but their on. A fact Six was quick to point out, particularly to Chanel, who now was attempting to hold back the smile creeping o her face. She made an effort not give their rude and boastful Captain the joy of seeing her relieved. The last thing he needed, as far as she was concern, was for her to give him an excuse. To continue to treat her in the manner in which he did. That was completely unacceptable!

Her anger soon subsided and they peacefully entered to acquaint themselves. Six looked on, as he nodded with approval. The first introductions were made at a round dinning table in the far corner, opposite the hatch they entered. Sitting at the table, were two large women with tall behaves hairstyles. They appeared to be in their mid-forties and full of money, visible by the gaudy jewelry they wore. With them was one much younger woman in her twenties. She was shy, quiet and spoke only when asked a direct question. She appeared to be very disinterested in the one-sided conversation and she smiled on queue only as a courtesy. Her eyes were red and puffy. They displayed either the sadness of a broken heart, fear or both.

Stach walked with Chanel on his arm to the table and slowly offered a friendly greeting.

"Hi sonny." replied the large lady on the front side of the table.

The others with her also paid their respects with an equally pleasant acknowledgement. "Please sit down darling, there's two sit here. Unless we're going auction a dinner for two with two tastefully full figured sweetie pies like us, who are looking for a good time!" joked the jolly woman with a huge warm smile about her face. Everyone joined in the laugh. "Well what are you waiting on honey?" she encouraged again moving the chair immediately next to her and patting the seat gently with her hand.

Stach lifted Chanel's hand and twisted her around carefully directing her into the empty spot. He walked around to take the chair next to the young woman with the sad eyes. Before he sat, she voluntarily moved one seat over to allow him to sit next to Chanel. He politely thanked her before he too seated.

"So honey, what's your name?" asked the joking women looking at him seductively up and down.

"Stach. Stach Wilson. And this is my fiancée Chanel Parker." he acknowledged, warmly putting his arm around her to minimize any idea of the woman might have had to continue flirting with him.

"Oh, isn't that sweet" she happily sighed. "Well, I'm June Roundly. Don't think about laughing, she said pointing her finger directly at him almost touching his nose. "I know I got plenty. Round that is!"

"You can say that again!" interjected the equally as round woman, sitting next to her."

"You shut up. That's Patty. Patty Melt." she replied as she screamed laughing, slapping herself on the knee. "I'm just kidding. Ooh Lord, I'm just too much fun."

"Yeah. You're a real riot." commented the other woman who was not thrilled about the implication of the joke.

"I'm sorry Patty. Stach, that's Patty Johnson. And this little young pretty thing here is Marie Harris, referring to sad eyes who was quietly trying to hold back her burst of laughter. "We came aboard for a little vacation. Marie's daddy die last month and we thought it would be a good idea to get away for awhile. Patty is my sister from Kentucky. Marie lives in Wyoming and is my niece. I'm of course am a proud Texan. Unfortunately, we don't get a chance to see each other often. After the funeral, I knew it was time to change that.  My brother was what you might call the glue that held us together. Since he's gone, I thought I'd be the one to take up the slack. He was certainly big on family values." she painfully reflected as tears began to roll up in her eyes.

"Come on you big turd, don't do that." her sister playfully said to lighten things up. The past month had been a difficult time for them. Patty somehow was able to stand strong, although June would disagree and always gave the impression she was the one who had the strength of steel.

The mood was changing. Chanel signaled with her eyes indicating to Stach it was time to move on. She still felt badly about the loss of their love one and wanted to perform a song for them at some point during their voyage.

"June, did you know my fiancée was an excellent

musician.

"Is that right darling?" she replied wiping the tears from her eyes, smearing the black mascara creating raccoon eyes.

"Yes madam and a very good one he is. He plays the saxophone. I'm somewhat of a singer myself. Maybe you will allow us to perform for you ladies some day before our trip is over."

Stach nudged her sharply on the leg. She felt his touch and knew it's meaning. Performing live for others was not his desire these days. His playing was strictly to satisfy his own therapeutic needs. It had become an intimate monogamous relationship between he and his instrument.

"That very sweet of you both. We would love to hear you sing. Wouldn't girls?" All simultaneously agreed. "So when are you going to do us the pleasure. Hopefully, very soon but not before I catch me a man. That's the other reason we came on this cruise. They said we were invited to be apart of a grand singles tour, and there would be a gang of available studs for us to choose. But from the look of things, we have the best this going already sitting here. No offense my dear" she said, lightly touching Chanel on the arm.

"Too late, he's already taken." she replied returning the pat on the hand. "I guess we'll move about and try to meet a few other guests before we retire for the night. Or should I say morning. This midnight departure has gotten me all disoriented. Anyway, it was a pleasure meeting you. We hope to see all of you again real soon."

"Sure you will. We're on a boat, where can we go?" The rest of the table said their good-byes and expressed delight at the acquaintance, "Don't forget about our song. We'll be expecting it!"

"Alright, you have a pleasant night." They stood and dismissed themselves. Then signaled for the first available waiter, to quench their enormous thirst with a glass of champagne. The toast was brief and the glasses emptied even quicker. They moved on to the couple standing adjacent to the bar, who appeared to be in high spirits. Free of hang-ups that would spoil the late festive atmosphere.

Chanel signaled again for one more drink to sociably take with them. With drinks in hand, they eased themselves into the conversation by lifting their glasses in gesture of a toast.

"Here's to a wonderful trip of love. May you all find as much love as your own hearts can possibly stand. Here. Here."

Each glass touched one another and a collective responding cheer rang in the air. "Here. Here."

Having broken the ice, Stach introduced he and Chanel. This time the conversation was more equally yoked and preceded smoothly.

"Mr. Mendell, how long has it been since you moved from Australia and started pursuing your new life in New York?"

"Oh Mate, it's been almost ten years if I've counted correctly. Seems like only yesterday, if I had to put a feeling on it. Guess that what happens when you're a late bloomer like myself."

His ascent was still heavy and the words rounded. Since his transition a decade ago, the East Coast climax had taken the reddish tan from his skin. His blond hair was still shoulder length but now sported traces of gray. Time however, still had been gentle to him over the forty years of his life. He stood tall and handsome with deep dreamy blues eyes. Muscles still filled his fame from all the years of hard labor on the family farm.

"How do you like it there? They tell me that's a pretty big apple to take a bit out of."

"An understatement in deed Mate. I try to keep it quiet for myself. I'm one who's not much for the big city trappings. Hey, I don't don't really like having all the money. I've brought me and the little wifey here, a nice big quiet spot in one of the New Jersey townships across the bridge. As far away from the city as I could get. Our house almost reminds of the farm I grew up in Australia. Now the Misses, she's a true New Yorker."

He looked into her eyes and softly rubbed her face with the outer tips of his fingers. She returned a warm smile, as she palmed his cheek with her hand. "I can't seem to keep her away from all that stuff." he continued. "Every night it's a different party, a different engagement, a different reason. In fact mate, I even offered to buy her a place over there, so we wouldn't always have to make the two-hour drive."

"Stop that sweetheart." interrupted the soft sexy voice of the woman in which he spoke of. "Don't give these nice people the impression I'm some kind loose party animal. I just enjoy the culture." she purred.

Stach took one more look at her sensuous body, seducing eyes, and jazzy attitude. He knew York had his hands full. They continued the conversation for awhile longer, before they realized that the night was quickly beginning to give way to the morning light.

"I'm afraid it's time for us to excuse ourselves and turn in for the rest of night. At least, what's left of it." announced Stach, eager to do nothing more than get hands around his sax. He desperately needed to play. Just one note would do.

"Damn! he exclaimed as they walk away. . He remembered it was still packed away in his luggage and their

26

belonging wouldn't be delivered until morning.

"What's wrong baby?"

"You what I like to do at night."

"Make love to me?" she said smiling while rubbing his butt and then giving it an inviting squeeze."

"That too, but you know what I mean."

"Oh that's right, we packed it away with our things.

"I told you we should have kept it with us, but you thought it would be too much trouble carrying it around. I knew I shouldn't have listened to you!"

"Look. Don't get angry with me. Everything would have worked out fine, if we hadn't gotten lost all this time. It's not my fault we got to wait until in morning. So get over it!"

As they exited, Six glanced and saw them leaving. He was standing near the hatch talking with a very young but strikingly attractive woman. Her hair was short and symmetrically cut and dyed pale red, which complimented her tanned bronze skin. She wore only flesh colored lipstick and black eyeliner to bring out her emerald eyes. Anymore makeup was not needed and would have only distorted the natural beauty she possessed.

Her father initiated the introduction. "Hey son. I saw you making your rounds. And Ms. Parker, I'm glad to see you have finally settled down." he acknowledged with a sarcastic grin.

"Don't flatter yourself." Her response was as sharp as a razor's edge.

"Well now. Don't get your feather's all ruffled. I'll like you to meet my darling little girl. I mean my daughter, Flower. Flower meet Ms. Parker. And this handsome gentleman here is Stach."

"Flower?" he thought what an appropriate name it was for a woman, whom exhibited the attributes of such a comparison should bear its name. Natural, beautiful, gentle and perfect in all of its parts. "That's a lovely name." he smiled slyly with lustful eyes. He then felt a jolt in his right side. "Oh." he painfully exhaled without looking in the direction from which the blow came. Its origin he knew. The pain settled and he stared no more.

"Hello Stach." she said returning her own flirtatious smile, while her eyes moved about his body, pausing briefly at the budge growing in his pants. She raised her eyebrow before lifting her eyes to meet his.

"Flower, is it?" the voice was cunning and venomous as only a woman could.

"Yes." the reply came quick.

"I'm Chanel. Stach's fiancée."

"My, I'm sorry I didn't know you were. You know, together."

"You mean a couple." she assisted, aware of the woman's surprise that this handsome white man would take up with a Negro woman. Regardless if she had exemplary qualities. "I know you didn't." she agreed with a tight-eyed look in her direction.

"That's not what I mean."

"Like father, like daughter." she mumbled under her breath.

The conversation moved to Six's intentions in bringing her along. As he talked, he was sure to bounce around the specific nature of his decision. Explaining she was whispered to be the town Jezebel. And himself had viewed her innocence being taken by the tongue of a teenaged boy, was not something he could easily reveal.

"Folks you ain't going to leave now are? Why don't you stay a little awhile longer and have a drink with me and Flower."

"Yeah, please. I've met a lot people on the ship and you two seem to be the only ones who's not out there!" she said pointing to here head with her index finger and twisting it. Stach turned to Chanel with a playful grimace. "Baby." he crooned hugging her close to his body.

"Come on!" Six insisted wrapping everyone into his gigantic arms. They relocated to the empty seats behind them. Six excused himself and strolled to the bar, which was no more than ten paces away. He eagerly pushed the bartender out of his path. They watched as he mechanically reached up and down, in and out preparing the five drinks with craftsman like precision. He returned proudly to serve them. Carefully, he selected each and placed it in front of its recipient. They made a collective toast.

"Whew! What do have in here? Battery acid!" said Stach, as he coughed and a grabbed his throat.

"Only for color my boy. Only for color." he laughed with the assurance he had set his special mix in the right place.

Stach endured the burning until it finally gave way to just an uncomfortable numbness which subsided to a mild sting when he attempted to gently swallow. Chanel and Flower smiled as they tenderly brought their own drinks to their lips and easing them over the brim of fragile gold tip brim. To each of their surprise the sips were pleasantly gentle. Easy to take in. The two women looked at one another and laughed as the realized Six's obvious intentions.

"Not too strong is it sweetheart?" Chanel asked, smiling

at Stach's reluctance to answer.

"Very funny, darling. What's up next? A side show!"

"That's what you get for insisting to provoke an argument about that saxophone of yours."

"Is that what this is really all about, the music? Excuse me, but I'm certain it was the music, which brought us together. Therefore to ignore its significance in our lives and blame it for what's wrong with us is completely unfair."

"Yes, I know! My dear if you think the music is why my heart has been empty without pulses of the right feelings and emotions."

"Love is more than an emotion!"

# THE POET'S
## Corner

*where the written word lives...*

title: the season
poet: j. Michael hicks


People come into our lives for a reason, season, or lifetime
I'm not trying to rhyme, maybe it was his time
The contemplation was on my mind
A reason, season, or lifetime
Strange how we work so hard for money
Over the smallest things we act funny
Has life passed us by
We have the nerve to pray and ask God why
A reason, season, or lifetime
The message is in his word
Be a verb, choose
Freedom and fly
Can't love one another like you're shy
Emotionally I try, before it happened did he cry
A reason, season, or lifetime

title: Acapulco eve
poet: j. michael hicks


A simplex of smile
Smooth, gentle breeze
With the dimples of a charmer
A cute, jazzy at ease
Flirtatious with your tease
Your hair I squeeze
It was the setting of an Acapulco eve

title: untitled
poet: a friend


She glanced at me,
Perhaps with envy.

She smirked at me,
Like she had a secret.

She can taste me,
Only on his lips.

She can' let go,
And she can' hold on,

Wanting... feel his body
Wanting ... kiss on the lips
Wanting... what she cant quite get

Except...
The taste of me on his lips

title: essence
poet: j. michael hicks


The essence of a woman
Can never be misunderstood
Then I saw you walking one day and breathless I stood
Uptown and in the neighborhood

The essence of a woman
Defined by plenty of measures and standards
Too many hard to find
I count honesty, communication, love and beauty as some of mine
Might sound traditionalized but I analyze before I socialized

The essence of a woman
Came through in your eyes and conversation
Heard in your words someone who wanted liberation
I can' change frustration you had in past relations
I come as the holy spirit offering salvation

The essence of a woman
Help me understand more
You I would adore and explore
While I build our love from the ground floor

The essence of a woman
Was easy to see
The essence of *that* woman made such an impression on me

title: untitled
poet: afriend


Her lips on my body
my body on him
She likes the taste of my pussy cat
Licking me
Sucking me
Put me on my knees
watch me suck your dick
And my ass is being licked
This is what I like
This is what's good to me
Tasting her with my tongue
Put your finger in my ass
This is what I want
This is what we want
The time is near

title: your game
poet: j. michael hicks


I hear your game
From your sexy brown legs I'd start
First I got to go through your heart
Love your mellow mood and your smart remarks
My tongue creeping starts
Slowing licking everywhere you part
Your body leaves those wet marks


I hear your game
If freaking you while you stand
Is all you got plan
Then I guess I can understand
Second thought, I ain't that kind of man
Build you a castle in the sand
Before any of that began


I hear your game
Your mind first, be spiritually diverse
Makes your heart thirst, then our bodies burst
I'm screaming hold me tight
Contemplations mean might
If we went to war, would you fight


I hear your game
Hum...anyway , what's your name
I won't tell, they don't know you well
Big world, small minds makes the thinking lame
Ssshh.....so can I hear your game

I proudly introduce a special poem from my 14year son, Jeremy. I love you.


title: my baby
poet: jeremy de'vaughn hicks


Baby you have been treating me bad
The day has past since I said I'm sorry for the sadness I've caused
Unmarked promises I put in the place of the sadness will soon be gone
Baby I plan to prove to you my dear
How much I truly care and if you think I've never loved you
Just know that I really do
I'd do anything for you baby
You just don't know
Tell me you love me and hold me so
I can't wait to see you by my side
To just hold you and see you smile
Tell you that I love to see you smile
Baby I am your cheese dino dude
And baby you know you're my cheese world
I just can't wait to kiss you
I'd put someone flat on their back
If they ever disrespected you
I'll hold you and love you so
Baby I'm sorry, but now I got to go